Twisted Paradise

Natasha Dreyfus

Contents

Prologue

T he night sky was shrouded in darkness tonight. There was no moon in sight to brighten her path. Even the street lamps glowing in the bleak setting were far in between.

Maybe the sense of gloom, the suffocating air of morbidity, had reached around her, blending in with her surroundings, sucking away all vitality.

Or maybe shame was eating away at them all. Maybe they couldn't show her their faces. Maybe they regretted watching but not taking any action.

Maybe they hated their helplessness.

She certainly did.

She didn't exhaust her mind further on that particular train of thought, instead, kept a single-minded focus on the next steps that her scarred, frail legs would take while trying to see with the handful of light offered as a charity and taking care to not step on sharp stones.

Sweat poured down her forehead and her back. Even though goosebumps erupted on her skin from the night's chill, she burned inside. She couldn't seem to get enough air in no matter how fast she breathed in and out.

Her body was heavier and heavier.

Her legs trembled but showed no signs of faltering. Even if her body was on the verge of giving up, she was determined to keep going by borrowing the strength of her mind. Since she was running away, since she was escaping, she would do it till the end was near.

On a rare moonless night, as coolness descended with the arrival of winter, nobody took note of the wild-eyed young girl running with a crazed vigour, like her life was dependent on it.

They would never know that ironically enough, it possibly did.

Chapter 1

In most fairy tales, the princess was sweet, pure and kind.

When the monsters came to take her away, she persevered through it with her compassion and goodness.

Then her magnanimous, graceful saviours came in and swept her out of those nightmares. Be it a Fairy Godmother, a charming Prince or even seven freaking dwarves, they all came to the rescue.

Heck, even monsters and beasts were after her pure, innocent soul.

They were sincere.

Their kind smile and friendly eyes were all real.

They never saved her to use her for their gain. The Princess never had to worry that she may just be escaping one monster to run into another.

Because in fairy tales, the Prince never turned out to be a monster. Because in fairy tales, the monsters turned into handsome princes for her.

Because she was kind. Because she was good.

And to Lily, among all the lies fed to children, that was the most unbearable and unforgivable one.

And so she arrived at the house she had been watching for quite some time.

The light was pouring out from the shutters of a single window while the rest of the duplex house seemed abandoned. Haunted.

Perhaps, because the owner himself was haunted?

The household staff were given an early leave. The lady of the house fell down the stairs and was severely injured, resulting in an immediate transfer to the hospital by her anxious husband. The two daughters accompanied their mother, deeply worried.

That's what people thought.

Lily stared up at the open window, striding towards the house.

No one knew that the man they praised as a loving husband beat his wife to the brink of death.

Twenty years of marriage and yet, she still hadn't managed to give him a son. The two daughters of his, he could barely bear. After all, what were they good for in his eyes except being traded away for marriage? He had no heir. That darn woman didn't manage to give him one.

Of course, that stupid man conveniently ignored how it was his fault that he never had a son. He was the one with the Y chromosome.

Funny how that worked, huh?

Her feet moved silently across the trimmed grass as well as the smooth marble floor. There were cameras installed in different places, but she knew they had stopped functioning a while back.

The place surrounded by walls was shadowy, not that it fazed her.

She was all too familiar with the darkness - the man in the room above being a contributing factor.

She swept through the large living room. Even though there were broken vases and objects thrown about in a disorganised manner, she effortlessly went past them. Legs fitted with spandex, she was quick on her feet.

She went up the stairs and let herself into that one brightly-lit room.

A balding man in his late forties was sitting at the corner of his bed. A wad of cash was scattered around; he was counting them obsessively.

Head bowed down, he was yet to notice her.

She ambled to his window and closed them with a resounding thud. The sound brought the man out of his obsessive reverie. He flinched back and looked at her, wide-eyed.

"All that money would go to waste without a son to inherit it. What a shame, right?" She asked him, lips hooked in a smile.

"Who the heck-"

"Who am I?" She asked again, still smiling. "Let's see..."

She took a few steps towards him. Perching herself comfortably at the corner of the bed. Her long manicured nails dragged over the silk sheets - a cardinal sin sweeping against alabaster.

"Should I be sad or should I not be sad? You don't remember me, Enrique?" Lily murmured, gazing at him from below her dark, long lashes.

He was glancing around frantically - his fingers twitching to reach the phone a few feet away.

Lily reached out and took the phone before offering it to him with an amiable smile.

He froze.

He stared at her, then at the phone she offered. Reaching out a wrinkled hand, he grasped it. But it was powered off. It wouldn't turn on.

"You should invest in a more secure phone, you know. The virus that infiltrated it..." She sighed in despair. "Your hand has nothing but a useless block of metal, now."

There was a deafening crash as the phone was thrown violently across the room, breaking several glass showpieces in the process.

She inwardly winced.

Those looked pretty expensive.

Enrique's face went from sickly pale to the colour of ripe tomatoes as realization barged in like an ostentatious group of burglars. "You bitc-"

"Now, now. I know I'm not one to talk but really, Enrique, violence and name-calling aren't the answer," she gently coaxed. "I mean, maybe if you focused less on anger and more on... well, healthcare, you might get a son."

"The heck are you implying, you wh-"

He couldn't finish saying the degrading word as a wad of cash crumpled into a ball got wedged in his mouth at lightning speed. His eyes widened and he started gagging, trying to get the bundle out.

Lily looked at him, her eyes turning wild with fury. "I said, no name calling."

She watched him for a few minutes as he finally got it out of his mouth.

"Our Capo already prepared for this situation, Ruby Wraith. Now that my phone is powered off, he's going to send men for me," he sneered, leaning his huge form forward as if hoping to overwhelm her.

Meh. She'd seen better.

Lily casually tapped a lean finger against her lower lip, organizing her features to a look of contemplation. "Hmm... you think the Capo would mind salvaging a corpse?"

"The men will be here in five minutes."

She smirked. "I could kill you in less than one."

But that was beside the point. That phone he threw was just a copy of the real one that was currently in her maroon blazer pocket. She had swapped it earlier when he wasn't looking.

Not to mention, just as a side precaution, she had set their warehouse ablaze. Surely the Capo would be busier trying to stop the fire and salvage their newly mass-produced meth?

Needless to say, those men Enrique was relying on weren't coming any time soon.

She would take her sweet time with him.

"What grudge do you have against the Giovanni Family, woman? I don't even know you!" His rage erupted like a volcano, confidence short-lived.

"Grudge? Against the Giovanni Family?" She stood up, eyes widening in astonishment. "I don't have a grudge against the Giovanni Family."

Her lips curled up, bold and beautiful, as she neared him. He stood up in alarm, taking steps back.

Eyes following his every step like a predator tracking its prey, she said, "But I do have a score to settle with you, young master."

The hair on his arms stood up as she uttered the last words. His pupils dilated. Lips drained of colour. Hands clenched into fists so tight, blood might pour out.

There was cautiousness in his eyes. And disbelief.

Her forest green eyes blinked with a touch of innocence, the corners of her lips tilted up in a bashful smile. "Do you not remember me, young master?"

The room was stiflingly quiet as the demons of his past flashed through his eyes. It was a well-lit room, yet, his breathing laboured as if there was only a haze of murkiness.

"You don't remember your Rose?" Eyes glassy with tears, she looked fragile as she glanced down at her red-black apparel. "Is it because I haven't dressed up as a pretty pink princess for you? Or maybe because I dyed my hair black? Do you prefer me blonde?"

"You..." His eyes were blown wide. Skin, a sickly pale. "You should be dead."

"You left me for dead, young master. You left me." Tears now streamed down her cheeks like an avalanche of pain. She took one tentative step and reached out a trembling hand towards him.

He flinched back, eyes haunted.

Like a madman. Like a man eaten up with his guilt. Like a man afraid of the monsters in his closet. The monsters under his bed.

Just like she had been.

She repressed the smile of satisfaction.

"Do you know how abandoned I felt? Used and discarded?" she murmured, voice trembling, almost breaking. "Do you know how I crawled out of the wasteland you threw me in? It was a dirty place, young master. It was a disgusting place."

Lily shoved her hand forward, hitting him on the chest. He fell backwards. He tried to escape, to ward her off but the drugs she had been sprinkling his food with for the past few months had gradually weakened his body at a natural and undetectable pace.

Even if she wasn't trained in martial arts, he would have been defenceless against her.

His hands moved about crazily on the cold floor. Whenever he tried to get up, she raised her foot to press on his chest, forcing him to stay down. He could only sweep back until she had him cornered against a wall, backed with no route of escape.

And looking down at him, Lily remembered. She remembered the girl with eyes full of stars. Eyes that knew hope and trust. Eyes that believed.

She also remembered the feeling. The feeling of her heart plummeting, eyes dimming, body trembling.

She remembered the darkness descending like a thick, foggy cloud.

She remembered being cornered. The wall behind her was just as white. White like innocence - something she was going to lose. The floor, as cold, had sent shivers through her tiny frame...

"Please..." the girl - the child - had pleaded with big watery eyes and wobbling lips.

"It's 'young master', my little Rose." The licentious voice had sounded. "Beg me and I might make it hurt less..."

All that and more, Lily remembered all too well.

She let loose that wild smile she'd been oppressing and lightly ran her bright red nail over his arms and legs, as his trembling increased.

Getting out a long silk tie, magenta in colour, she gently fixed it on him. "Remember how you tied up my hands with a replica of this? When I saw this online, I just had to buy this, you know."

He couldn't do anything except tremble more as his voice left him long ago, and she wanted to rage at how pathetic he looked. Instead, she gave him a warm smile and pressing one long leg on his chest, she viciously pulled the tie.

His hand clawed at the tie around his neck as his mouth gaped open in hopes of the slightest bit of air. His eyelids started fluttering as a slow glazed look came to his eyes.

Much as she hoped to look like an avenging angel in his fading vision, she was pretty sure that she looked more like a disturbing demoness.

She only released her grip when his skin started showing a tint of blue. And he gasped, trying to suck in dear old oxygen from the air around him.

Before he fully caught back his breath, she pulled on the tie, once again, calmly studying his skin, waiting for the familiar blue hue.

"You've been quiet for so long. Beg me, young master, and I might make it hurt less..." she cooed at him, a bright smile painted on her lips, but her strength as she pulled on the tie did not lessen.

She was planning on giving every pint that he had given her back. No one could argue she wasn't generous.

She'd probably be here for more than an hour.

A sigh escaped her.

She was so going to hit the bar with Selene later on.

Chapter 2

W ith a book in hand, the ice blonde who looked far too young took small measured sips of wine from her glass. Her eyes were glued to the open pages, the only indication of her reading being the slight movement of her pupils as it went over the letters. Her eyes were the colour of a frozen arctic lake that never thawed and her pale face, smooth as jade, held no expression; not even a light furrow between the eyebrows.

Lily removed her left hand from her face and rested her cheek on the right one, still looking at the woman in front of her. They came here to loosen up and have some fun. But, of course, Selene was above such vulgarity - as she called it.

The bar was dimly lit, blaring music drowning out all other sounds. Looking at the people on the dance floor, that congested place had bodies all squashed to each other, moving along with the tempo, abandoning all inhibitions.

Hair flying all over; wandering hands. Intoxicated, glazed eyes.

In contrast to that, Selene was a white flower framed with soft, snowy petals and an angelic halo glimmering around her. Separated from the ugliness of the world, it made one feel ashamed to look at her. As if when exposed to others for too long, the shine will lessen and she will start to taint.

Adorable and pure. Lily rolled her eyes. As if.

Turning her head, she called over the bartender. Well, it was mostly her crazy hand-flying motion that caught his attention, considering even she couldn't hear herself over the ear-splitting noise.

"Another glass, miss?" A dimple formed on his right cheek as he smiled. His messy brown curls splayed about and the impertinent arch of his eyebrows promised thrill and adventure.

Her lips quirked. She opened her mouth to answer--

"I'll be paying for this young lady's next drink."

--That... wasn't what she was going to answer.

She whipped around her head, a range of colourful words to say to this guy - couldn't he see she was trying to flirt? Couldn't he sense it? - but they all got stuck in her throat the moment she took a look at him.

Now, appearance-wise?

He wasn't much.

So it wasn't his overwhelming beauty or anything like that which made her swallow the words.

This man was trying to appear suave, his greasy black hair slicked back to perfection. An expensive suit, coupled with a Rolex watch on his wrist. The sprayed cologne of money... he was hoping to score tonight.

She glanced around, seeing what else she could spot about this guy. She was avoiding looking straight at him, sweeping forward her dark locks just so they would hide half of her face.

"Does the lady accept?" he asked with a smile that seemed lecherous to her.

She wanted to slap him.

Then again, everything this man did appear lecherous to her. So she might be just a tad bit biased.

"I never say no to a free drink," she said, raising a playful eyebrow, attempting to appear composed instead of frayed at the edges that she was inside. There must have been a slight faltering in her tone somewhere because she had the feeling of a pair of eyes on her back.

Seemed like Selene finally managed to tear herself away from her book.

Lily wanted to turn her head back to look at her but she didn't want the guy to get even a whiff of her unease.

What was he doing here? Shouldn't he be busy with his Capo trying to minimize the damage her fire caused? Didn't Enrique's corpse get discovered yet?

What the heck was he doing here?

This wasn't fair. She wasn't mentally or emotionally prepared.

She wasn't ready.

"You seemed familiar across the bar." The guy was now studying her curiously.

Her blood ran colder than the coldest night.

Of course.

Even though how she looked now was a world apart from the scrawny girl he used to know... little similarities would always remain.

She forced out a somewhat convincing laugh. "I think I'd remember you if that happened." She slowly looked him up and down in a teasing manner, getting more into the act - her familiar domain. "You aren't exactly a hard-to-miss kinda guy."

He was convinced for the moment, male ego and all. But what about later? What if this thought perked up again in the future?

Like, in the shower! Didn't people always have random earth-shattering shower thoughts at the most unexpected of times?

(No? Only her, then? Whatever.)

Lily had worked so hard to come to this point. She wasn't about to risk it being thrown into disarray because of a careless mistake; a moment of miscalculation.

So as she chugged down the drink he'd bought her, she arranged her features in a way that made her olive complexion glow. Her scarlet-painted lips stretched up in a lopsided smirk, highlighting the beauty mark above her lip - the right side of her face. Her eyelids slightly dropped down, the dark long lashes fluttering, giving the impression of sinful eyes clouded with intoxication.

Her vulnerable condition brought forth a glint in the guy's eyes; a predator's glint. His hand reached out and enveloped her imperceptibly calloused one. "You want to get out of here?"

Woah.

That was fast.

Oh well. She could only blame herself for being too good at acting. Poor her.

Still, her smile deepened. "Please. This crowd's killing me. Really need some air."

He stood up and pulled her up along with him. Drunk as she was, she was a bit unstable on her feet and being the nice guy he was, he snaked an arm around her waist to stop her swaying.

He even coped a feel, that lecher.

She bit back the revulsion.

As they left the bar, him half-carrying her, she made sure to meet Selene's eyes with her no longer clouded but sharp ones.

Lily didn't think he'd save her the effort and lead her towards an alley himself. But then again, she really should have expected it from someone like him.

The corner they were in was dark and isolated. In his dark outline, the only thing flashing was his beady eyes - the lust in them taking her back... back to before...

"Listen to 'young master' if you don't want it to hurt, sweet Rose," his voice had whispered in a disgusting purr.

Damn it.

She clenched shut her palms, the long sharp nails digging into the rough flesh, the pain of it keeping her from drifting to a place where no one could reach her. A place she wouldn't be able to come back from.

She was pushed against a choppy wall. She hoped her back didn't get scratched too badly.

She watched him come closer, the predatory light in his eyes brewing stronger than a typhoon, staying right where she was, not moving an inch.

At least, not that he could see. But one of her hands had already wrapped around the silent revolver in her purse.

This entire thing wasn't carefully planned. But she had to take this step to stop any future entanglements. After wiping Lorenzo out, she knew there would be one hell of a cleaning to do.

Selene would be pissed.

With a fresh murder just a few hours ago, she couldn't afford to be careless but also, she couldn't let this guy go and risk her failing at the last second!

Trapped between a rock and a hard place, that's what she was. And the world was, as always, unfair to her. And she couldn't run away. Lord knew how badly she wanted to.

He was only a breath away, now. Both of his hands slammed against the two sides of the wall, caging her in between. That, along with his large physique, he easily loomed over her like a ghoulish silhouette.

But she wasn't nervous.

This idiot left a sizable amount of gap between their bodies. It wouldn't take much effort to--

The body was suddenly torn from her, the air she breathed becoming less toxic.

The stench of freshly-spilt blood travelled towards her right after she heard the mighty crack of a skull crushed against the gravel.

"Am I interrupting?"

Oh, for heaven's sake. Who the hell was it this time?

Chapter 3

"Are you alright, miss? I saw him drag you here and you looked pretty drunk, so I grew worried..." A smooth and polite voice; one that sent shivers down her body though not the unwelcome kind.

The newcomer glanced at the dead Lorenzo on the ground.

"You know me...?" asked Lily, secretly releasing her grip on the revolver; it was no longer needed.

There was a smile mingled in his tone. "Do I need to know someone to help them? The world would come to an end if that was the case."

Her world had already come to an end, long ago. This must've been why.

She closely stared at him. The darkness didn't allow her to pinpoint his features but she could see he was tall and lean. His stance was sophisticated and exuded an abnormal amount of confidence.

He had managed to swiftly deal with Lorenzo. And his tone, so far, did not betray any hint of anxiety or trepidation at what he just did.

In her experience, normal people tended to be a little fussy about people dying, more so committing murder, for some reason.

But he didn't seem to be affected. Either the situation still did not sink in for him - which she didn't think was the case - or...

Swift as a bullet, she made up another plan.

Killing with a borrowed knife was better in her current situation... that is if the borrowed knife didn't turn out to be blunt.

"I-Is he dead? He was seen with me last, what if this gets out and... and..." her voice was shaky as if the thought of what would follow took a great toll on her.

"No need to worry about that." He gave an indifferent shrug. "Rest assured, I will take care of it. For now, please follow me out."

As they slowly walked out of this isolated place and towards lit-up streets, he kept a cautious amount of distance between them.

Trying to make her feel safe, perhaps? She experienced a traumatizing event just now, after all.

(Or so it seemed.)

... but why make the effort? Was he planning on giving it his shot as well, later on? Trying to lower her guard so he can jump on her when she least expected it?

She took out her phone from her purse and sent Selene a text before keeping it away.

They were back on the streets by now. The bar she had gone to was in front of her. She turned herself to finally get a clear look at him.

... And all words got stuck in her throat for the second time this night.

On second thought, maybe she wouldn't mind if he tried giving his shot. Gladly welcome him, even. It felt like those terrible fairy tales fed to children where the curse was lifted and a handsome Prince was there at their call.

(Though she was pretty sure this one had an ulterior motive.)

The lights shone on his face, accentuating his high cheekbones. A spray of light freckles powdered his nose; a galaxy of stars waiting to be explored. Tendrils of his dark hair wove in and out of one another resembling the waves on a turbulent sea. They overflowed out of the crest of his head and she wondered if they would feel as soft as they looked were she to delve her fingers into those silky strands.

His eyes were like the fog on a winding road, blurring her vision and mysteriously muddling her sense of direction. Its mahogany shade was calming, yet the ruthless glint in them warmed up her blood, making her lightheaded. She was trapped in the tantalizing danger they promised as if she was on drugs.

Was she on drugs? Who was this beauty she met for the first time today?

The aforementioned beauty raised an elegant eyebrow at her blatant staring. Relentless eyes still as ferocious. Rosebud lips curled in a languid smile. "Am I handsome?"

"Oh, Absolutely gorgeous."

His eyebrow went higher.

How the hell did he manage to make that look attractive?

"Not holding back, I see." He had a soft and friendly expression as if he had nothing to hide, and looking at him, she felt inexplicably at ease.

"I came here with my friend." Her head tilted helplessly. "But she's probably gone by now. We were supposed to have dinner together before leaving."

Well, not really. But what was freedom of speech for if you didn't use it to lie?

"You must be hungry then. Let me treat you to dinner?" She was being pretty obvious in wanting to dine with him. Yet, he phrased his answer as a request.

She beamed at him in acquiescence.

His manner of walking was unhurried as if he had all the time in the world in his hand and he couldn't be bothered to make more of an effort. Anyone looking at him would feel automatically relaxed.

As they entered the restaurant, the staff who saw him turned pallid. It was like they encountered death itself and were simply dying - pun absolutely intended - to flee with their lives.

Instead, they got more cautious with their work, displaying their impressive skills to the fullest.

A middle-aged waiter came to them trying to hide the expression of a soldier running off to join a losing battle.

"Welcome back, sir!" he said, but the smile on his face shook so vigorously that Lily was tempted to ask him if he was planning on shedding. "Would you like a private room as per usual?"

"A private corner will suffice, this time." He glanced at her to see if she was okay with it.

She gave an approving nod.

And so they moved towards a quiet corner; a table off to the side that was giving the illusion of privacy but the other people were still in her peripheral vision. As they got closer, he pulled the chair back, gesturing at her to sit.

Lily looked at the chair he pulled back for her and looked at him.

Then with a slight chuckle of disbelief (because why bother?), she firmly sat down on it, one leg draped over another.

He gazed at her, who was brimming with mischief, the curiosity in his eyes softening the ruthlessness. A slight curl at the corner of his lips. "What's so funny?"

"First time having a chair pulled back for me."

"Oh? What sort of men have you been accompanying?" The curl of his lips turned teasing.

"The normal ones?"

A low magnetic chuckle. "Miss... Are you calling me abnormal?"

"It's Lily. Call me Lily."

"Lily..." He glanced at her, tilting his head to the side, with a look of contemplation. It made him seem enigmatic. "Lovely name."

"This is the point where you reciprocate with your name, saviour of mine," she pointed out helpfully, leaning towards him with an arched eyebrow. A smile, sly and sensual, painted her scarlet lips.

The mild smile that bloomed on his face in return made her really miss oxygen because - damn - she sure wasn't getting enough of it at that specific moment.

So there was such a thing as breathtaking beauty. Here she was thinking the poets - those old geezers - were lying.

"Blaise," He said and gazed deep into her eyes as if searching for something.

Ah... oh...

"Blaise?" She asked slowly, not letting anything else colour her tone, keeping her eyes as veiled as possible. "A beauty called Blaise... that fits perfectly."

But he was still staring at her, scrutinizing. She didn't know what he was trying to see through her craze-filled eyes. But trying to do so never ended well.

Her eyes hardened.

Ever.

Just then the waiter arrived to take their orders.

The tense atmosphere building up steadily dissipated as she gave her order and watched him do the same.

He spoke as soon as the waiter left, "I'm sorry about earlier. I didn't mean to make you uncomfortable."

Well, she wouldn't go that far. She wasn't uncomfortable, just... on guard. She built back some of the shields that had gone down. Inadvertently.

She should thank him, really.

A small laugh escaped her lips. "What are you talking about? Why would I be uncomfortable? I hope you aren't uncomfortable that I called you a beauty."

An unnamed emotion blazed through his eyes at her answer, far too fast for her to grasp. But then those eyes went back to being relentless like a tempest on the sea and his expression was breezy, almost making her question if all that really happened; whether he was deluding her or she was deluding herself.

"Not at all... I am flattered to be noticed by another beauty," he said with a friendly smile.

She wouldn't trust him as far as she could throw him but, dammit, that cold-blooded gaze seared through her, turning her blood into lava.

How could a person with such a warm smile have such dangerously glinting eyes?

She took out her phone from her purse and held it out, looking straight at him.

"If you're flattered then write down your number for me."

I am very nervous about this chapter. After all, in a romance novel, a lot depends on the Male Lead.

What do you think of this Male Lead?

Did you like the interactions between Lily and Blaise?

I am so nervous!

Chapter 4

She didn't let him drive her home.

Until further research, his number - newly added to her phone - would have to be enough.

She got out of the taxi and stood in front of a tall building. The night was dark but the ground floor was well-lit. She walked through the door opened by the guard, her high heels on the marble floor causing a disturbance in the silence.

Easily opening the sleek black door due to the installed retinal scanner, Lily entered the penthouse she shared with Selene.

Its decor was luxurious; of ivory and silver. Under the bright lights, the entire place seemed to twinkle like stars, full of glitz and glamour.

She breezed into the living room.

Selene was reclined on the light velvet sofa with her legs tucked in a dainty manner. Her silver hair, let out of its bun, cascaded down her petite body. In her slender hands was that same damn book from earlier. Her full lips were pursed so slightly it would take someone studying her for years to be able to tell - but that was what Lily did.

Looking at this angelic ball of cuteness, Lily wanted to squeeze her squishy cheeks as much as she wanted to fling that book out the window. Both would annoy Selene equally so she found it difficult to decide.

"Did you go and check?" Lily asked her instead.

Raising her eyes from the book, Selene locked them with hers. In her eyes was a wintry night, cold and beautiful. It made a striking contrast to the rest of her sweet, delicate features.

Blaise was the same.

His expression was friendly and mild but his ruthless eyes showed his true nature.

"There wasn't even an iota of trace left in the alley by the time those men were done. Whoever you swindled this time was pretty capable."

Lily smirked at her. "He's expected to be. But his capability can be a blessing or a curse for me, depending on my choices. So do me another favour and look into Blaise Roosevelt. See what you can find other than the current circulating rumours."

Icicles forming in Selene's eyes were the only indication of her emotional state.

"Blaise Roosevelt... you really like playing with fire, don't you?"

Lily shrugged, unapologetic in her choices.

"Lilithe."

"Don't call me that, Selene."

"Not the time for you to chase after an adrenaline rush."

"You know me too well," she said with a devilish smile. "But I haven't fixated on anything, yet. Don't be too anxious."

Her playful eyes traced over the creamy complexion of Selene's face as she added, "Otherwise, you'll get wrinkles."

Selene's ice-blue eyes shuttered as the temperature in the room lowered drastically.

"Why do I bother with you..." she then muttered before picking her book up and promptly ignoring her.

She probably shouldn't have teased her about the wrinkles.

Lily needed to unwind after that long night. Her back was still mildly throbbing from being pushed against the wall earlier by that bastard.

She drew herself a warm bath.

Stepping into the bathtub, she let herself relax against the comforting warmth - her aching muscles being soothed. She didn t realize how tightly winded she was tonight until she felt all her stress evaporate away. Layers over layers.

In this state of contentment, her mind brought forth his name.

Blaise Roosevelt.

Back at the restaurant, she refrained from revealing her recognition of him. She didn't have all the facts at her disposal, yet. She didn't know how she would proceed. She didn't have a clear plan.

But she knew him.

She had a hunch about his identity from the moment she saw him. That grew stronger when she noticed the reactions of the restaurant staff.

And when he told her his name... only an idiot wouldn't connect the dots.

It was too obvious.

Therefore, she was sure he didn't buy her pretence of not recognising him. But he didn't seem to be suspicious of her either. From what she observed throughout, he seemed to think of her as a harmless woman.

Yet, if she somehow read him wrong or failed to correctly interpret his thoughts, then that man had some mad acting skills.

Then again, wouldn't it make perfect sense if he did? She would be concerned if he didn't. After all, Blaise Roosevelt was a Mafia boss. and the boss of the Italian Mafia wasn't someone to be taken lightly or recklessly.

Because she was almost certain he would run a background check on her as soon as he reached home. If she got his nature right.

(And she was always right.)

As a Made man, he was reputed to be ruthless and cold-blooded. He didn't know mercy and was unforgiving to his enemies.

He took over as the boss, exactly six years ago, after he stabbed his father to death. According to rumours, the promise of power made him muddle-headed. When he saw his father paying particular attention to another boy - some said it was the underboss - near his age, he snapped and lost control, fearing he would lose it all.

On that bleak night, there was a bloodbath, streaming and vibrant. His father's along with that boy.

He was only sixteen back then.

Lily herself saw the man just some time ago. She saw his chilling mahogany eyes. She saw the promise of peril in them. She could easily believe that he was ruthless and cold-blooded. She could easily believe that he was relentless to his enemies.

But because she saw the man just some time ago, she couldn't believe the rumours of him being blinded by power and snapping. He didn't strike her as the type of person who was impulsive and abrasive - one who so easily lost control.

Even if he stabbed his father to death, Lily didn't think it was because anger and fear blindsided him and his greed and insecurity got the best of him.

Yet, with his power and influence, he could easily stomp the news to the ground, so that not even their shadows remained. Since he didn't do so, she would guess it benefitted him to have his enemies underestimate him as a monster driven by bloodlust and give him an edge over those under him.

A little fear, after all, went a long way in gaining obedience.

In any case, she wasn't so stupid as to let rumours guide her perspective. There was a reason rumours and facts weren't synonymous words - rumours were often no more than cheap lies fed to the ignorant who had nothing else to do.

She knew that better than anyone.

"Breaking news: Ruby Wraith strikes again. Two victims this time."

Selene's monotonous voice wasn't the first thing Lily hoped to hear as she entered the dining room for breakfast. Their cook, Mrs Morelle, always put her heart and soul into preparing food for them and liked to nag at them to eat more.

But if Selene was bringing this up that meant she already left.

And sure enough, she was sitting in a corner with her laptop in front of her. Her gaze, glued to the screen. If Mrs Morelle were here, she would rant about the new generation and their harmful addictions.

"They linked me to his death?" Lily asked, taking a bite of her extra-spicy chicken.

Selene looked up at her, sending a withering glance. One that conveyed an insurmountable amount of disappointment over her deteriorating brain.

Ouch.

"After murdering five members of the Giovanni Family throughout the years and gleefully making it public, what did you expect, Lilithe? Whether you killed Lorenzo yourself or by borrowing a hand, you cannot escape suspicion. Did you lose your remaining few brain cells after the debacle last night?"

My, what a long paragraph.

Lily rolled her eyes at Selene's expression, reaching over to playfully tap her button nose. "You're so mean it breaks my fragile heart. And I told you to call me Lily."

Selene turned her head away in a disdainful manner before Lily could touch her and said indifferently, "I will call you Lily the day you call me Iclyn."

"But Selene suits you better!"

"Except, that is not my name."

"Well, I'm giving you that name."

"You are under no condition to be giving people anything. At the situation you have landed yourself in, you need only take, unrelentingly."

Right then, Selene gestured at her phone before it gave a ping. And she peeked at it to see an email from Selene.

"That is what I could get about him. I did not want to snoop too long and alert his men."

Selene excelled at computer science. She could hack her way into and out of programs without letting a single warning reach the owners. By the time she was done, nobody would be any wiser.

Whenever Lily planned each of her... cases, she would rely on Selene to provide her with the necessary information and deal with the electronics; security cameras and such.

Even though she would express her clear disdain every time... Selene never turned her away.

She was the only person in Lily's life who never turned her away.

Ever since the day Lily had met her and stared at her pleadingly with her wide child-like eyes brimming with hopelessness.

Selene had helped her when she herself was in trouble.

To this day, she continued doing so.

We officially meet Selene, or Iclyn as she'd want us to call her. What is your opinion of her?

More importantly, what do you think of that bit of info released on Blaise?

Chapter 5

When he arrived, Santano Giovanni, the Capo of the Giovanni Family, already getting the news of his killing of that ingrate named Lorenzo, had been waiting with his two soldiers.

Did he think killing Lorenzo was enough to vent his anger? Did he think he was safe, now?

Blaise blazed past him to his office, cold rage subtly taking over, as Santano and his soldiers followed like obedient dogs.

"Boss," he said, head bowed down, respectfully. "I will compensate for this accident. I will make you twice-no, thrice the money I've caused you to lose."

"Is it that easy?" Blaise asked, reclining in his seat, his eyes calmly inspecting the book in his hand. It was a classic - one he had read enough times for the spine to look worn out. "Do you know how much I lost because of this accident as you call it? Eight hundred million dollars."

Santano recoiled as if he had been shouted at or even hit. "It was Ruby Wraith. I'm sure of it. She killed Enrique while my men and I were at the warehouse-"

"And how did Ruby Wraith know the warehouse's location... Or was that another accident?" he asked softly, a mild smile on his face.

Santano looked down, not daring to comment, lest he digs his grave further.

At the resounding silence, Blaise peered at the two muscular men flanking Santano. His smile turned friendly but looking at him induced shivers in Santano's body. "Are they newly recruited? I have not seen them before."

Santano looked at the men at his sides, face blanched.

It was then a matter of seconds.

Multiple gunshots rang in the stillness of the night, one after another, giving no time for one to breathe or even let the situation sink in. Two huge bodies slouched and eventually crumbled down - bright crimson blood gushing out like a stream of overflowing water, filling the room with its fresh metallic stench.

Santano closed his eyes, kneeling on the ground and trembling, as blood from both sides splattered on his deathly pale face and tainted his beige shirt.

All this while, the soft smile on Blaise's face remained intact as if he was talking with a friend over tea, even as his eyes held a bloodcurdling expression.

He smoothly put away his gun.

"Maybe they should follow their erstwhile brother Lorenzo to the underworld to learn the trade, lest more such accidents take place in the near future."

The thick, loosely bound folder slid away from him. A disturbance amongst the otherwise neat mahogany desk.

His subordinates had slid away as well, while he was engrossed in reading its contents, albeit, less noisily.

Lilithe Blackthorne.

That was her name. But she told him to call her Lily. Yet, he preferred Lilithe.

Lily seemed too ordinary a name for a woman so exotic.

Moving away towards the all-encompassing glass walls, he would have been blinded by the light streaming in from the smouldering sun were his eyes not protected by the vision that had been refusing to leave him since yesterday night.

When he looked across his office room, out at the wide sky or even closed his eyes momentarily, she remained swimming in his vision.

Thick, sable locks of hair cascaded down her body, lustrous curls framing her face. Red lips, with a beauty spot at the top right corner of her lips, set in an impish smile, always contemplating her next adventure; the next thrill she would dive into.

He supposed she was someone who didn't like staying idle. Someone like her was always ready for fun.

Whispers in his ear sounded, telling him that her idea of fun probably consisted of something different than the ordinary and typical.

Her record was spotless, not even a speeding ticket, but that was the first red flag to look out for.

There were forests in her green eyes and looking into them too long made him afraid, very afraid, of losing his way and being trapped inside for life.

Staring into her eyes, one felt like they would be devoured whole until scraps, unimportant and inconsequential, were all that was left of them. And Blaise realized somewhere during their dinner together that this was intentional on her part.

She wanted her eyes to have this effect.

This woman wanted to run as much as she didn't want to run. She didn't want people to see through her. She didn't want the prodding and poking. It was easier to pretend.

The thought of being exposed scared her more than anything.

It scared her more than death.

He wondered how badly she would react if she found out that he saw through her.

Very badly, he then guessed.

Better if she didn't know then.

He wanted to help her, not traumatize her more than she already was - not that she showed it.

A light knock at his door drove him out of his reverie. The door soon opened to reveal a tall middle-aged woman. Her lips were stretched in a smile that promised warmth, eyes crinkling at the corners.

"Mom?" He rushed towards her, taking her by the arm and helping her sit on his chair. "Why didn't you tell me you were coming? I would have waited for you at the front door."

His mother sternly shushed him while trying to hide the twinkle in her warm eyes.

"I always want to see how my son is doing. But how can I disturb you every time?"

"I'm not disturbed if it's you."

"Such a silver-tongued son I have." Her lips turned up at the corners. She pushed against his forehead with a finger. "But I'm still not going to do it."

"Be honest, mom, you came because you got wind of the warehouse burning down, didn't you?"

She ignored him and instead glanced around his desk. Her eyes zeroed in on that file as her hand reached out and brought it closer.

"Lilithe Blackthorne," she read out loud. Then looking back at him, she asked in mock horror, "You're stalking girls now? Has my son turned into such a degenerate?"

Despite knowing she wasn't being serious, he was slightly offended at the degenerate part. The stalking part, however? He didn't know how else to explain away.

"It's not like you think, mom," he tried to explain. "I met her. Yesterday night."

Adding that last part might not have been the wisest decision he ever made because his mother's regal eyebrows raised a couple of inches in surprise.

"Night, you say? Don't tell me-"

"No, mom. I-Am I that type of man?"

He put a hand on his face which had heated up to an alarming degree. After a couple of seconds, a gentle hand removed his one from his face.

His mom was staring at him, finally serious.

Sort of.

"You met her and you were intrigued, is that it?"

He nodded, relieved.

"So you decided to breach her trust and privacy the first thing today?" She asked again.

He blinked. "I'm ninety-nine per cent sure she ran a background check on me as well."

She let out a little laugh. "Two peas in a pod, then?"

His mother looked at him fondly.

Her eyes were soft as velvet and warm as a fireplace. But he remembered a time when they had been filled with mental anguish and turmoil. Unconquerable anxiety. And trauma in bundles upon bundles.

They had been timid and terror-stricken. Petrified.

At a young age, they had scarred him, striking him deep like a stab wound on his flesh, in a way that blood-soaked clothes and purplish decapitated heads never managed to.

She used to look like she wanted to run, run away from the hell she was trapped in. But then, when she had looked at him, conflict swimmed in his mother's glassy eyes - the fight against that urge to flee.

She had wanted to run and not run at the same time.

Those tortured eyes always followed him around, stapled into his heart, and he never wanted anyone to have to feel that way. But that woman he met last night, that exquisite woman with an equally exquisite name, she had those exact same eyes - hidden behind a facade of craze and mischief.

He saw through the facade, when most people couldn't, because he knew what to look for.

And he knew if he didn't help her, if he pretended to not notice, and moved on with his life, he wouldn't be able to look at himself in the mirror ever again.

"Mom, it's just that... the look in her eyes took me back to those days, for a while." His mother's eyes turned sombre as he continued, "And after that, I couldn't simply walk away from her. Maybe I would have if I wasn't so familiar with the look in someone's eyes after they have been violated in the worst way possible."

He glanced down at his hands, clenched into fists, and slowly loosened them. "But I am familiar with it. My own mother suffered through this. How can I just walk past?"

A pale, warm hand rested on his slender, fair ones, giving them a light, comforting squeeze. He turned his head to peer at her and saw his mother's sparkling eyes.

"That's another reason you killed Lorenzo? Besides being angry about the money." At his nod, she continued, "You know, there aren't many things I'm proud of in my life. A lot of choices, I would do anything to take back. But having you as a son is the one thing I've never regretted."

Then taking in a deep breath and slowly releasing it, she regained her composure. Unbelievably fast.

"By the way," his mother said with an eager smile, standing up from the chair - ready to take her leave. "Be sure to bring her to me later on. Whatever the reason, she's the first woman you took interest in... ever. Who knows? Sparks may fly."

Blaise withheld the urge to let out a resigned sigh. "I will pretend I didn't hear that."

She pretended not to know his identity back when he told her his name. Despite her mostly fearless attitude, she must have some degree of wariness toward him.

Which was smart, he reasoned. If she were anyone else but herself, she'd have had ample reason to be wary of him.

But as it was, she did not need to be distrustful of him. He held no interest in tormenting a woman who had already been tormented so beyond his comprehension.

So his first mission would be to soothe that fiery spirit that held fears abound in its embrace and take down her ironclad guard. He needed to make her feel comfortable in his presence.

Only then can he work on helping her.

So... we uncovered some infomation in this chapter. The Giovanni Family who caused Lilithe so much trauma is actually working under him! Let me know how you feel about Blaise now.

Were you hoping he saved her wholeheartedly because he was such a sweet and decent boy?

And we met a new character! What do you think of his mom? XD

Chapter 6

It was a few days after that night and Lily had made up her mind. Men so dangerously alluring didn't fall from trees. She'd be stupid if she didn't take the chance to spend some time with him. And after a few weeks, when they both get bored, they'll separate and continue with their lives.

Simple enough. Like it had always been with her.

She was startled as her phone started ringing with the caller ID Straitlaced Max flashing. She had added 'straitlaced' before his name just to humour Selene as she kept insisting that it defined his entire personality. She wanted to tell Selene about the pot calling the kettle black but she knew that woman would argue that she was indifferent, not uptight.

She then sighed after ignoring the call. Okay, maybe the separation wasn't always so simple with her since this cop kept on calling her even after she ended it.

It was tough being so desirable.

Of course, Selene wasn't so happy with her decision. Lily could understand that. Blaise Roosevelt wasn't a joke. He was dangerous.

But that made her want to get involved with him even more.

She was bored.

She needed to be involved in something that would regularly guarantee a healthy dose of terror. Where one mishap could cost her a life. That was what made life riveting.

The perilous thrill.

Of course, trouble will come in all too readily if he discovered who she was.

... she needed to be extremely careful just so Blaise didn't suspect her to be Ruby Wraith. Even if Selene found no connection between him and the Giovanni Family, she was still technically killing those of his kind.

The result would be ugly if it got exposed.

She was snapped out of her bubble of thought as the bell ring sounded. Selene walked out to open it.

Lily quickly hid behind the silver-plated wall, in case it was one of her ex-boyfriends who didn't get the hint and insisted on pathetically chasing after her.

Yet, as Selene with her tiny frame opened the door, what awaited was the much taller, dark-haired, mahogany-eyed Mafia boss.

Now that was a surprise.

With hands in his pockets, his stance was laid-back. He gave Selene a polite smile which Lily was sure she didn't reciprocate.

Before he could say anything, Lily stepped away from the wall she was hiding behind and walked towards those two nonchalantly as if she was just passing by and happened to see them there.

"Just the man I was thinking of," she said, smirking as he rested his eyes on her. "What has he been up to these days?"

He shrugged, languidly.

"If I told you, I would lose my aura of mystery."

She led him to the drawing room and offered him a seat on the light velvet sofa. "Also, I'm not going to ask how you knew my address."

He raised an elegant brow after sitting down.

A friendly smile played on his lips as he asked, "Because you're the kind of person who let things go or because you already know?"

It was her turn to shrug, though not nearly so languidly.

"Answering that would lessen my aura of mystery." She winked playfully as his smile widened.

And then Selene entered the room as well but plopped down on a different sofa. Picking up the opened book beside her with a dainty hand, she continued reading from where she left off.

Catching Blaise's curious gaze on the living ice sculpture, Lily dramatically leaned towards him to whisper, "Selene's reading a romance novel like she always does twenty-four per seven. Even though she doesn't outright show it, I know she goes crazy for those fictional male leads."

"I can hear you, Lilithe. Stop stage-whispering," Selene remarked with an expressionless face, arctic blue eyes still on the novel.

Lily tried not to roll her eyes again as an involuntary smile crawled to her lips. At this point, her eyes would roll out of their sockets before the year was over.

She pulled Blaise up after standing up herself and more or less dragged him to the airy balcony with the view of the city below it. The temperature was too cold in that room.

"What about you? Do you read?" he asked, tilting his head to the side in a way that made a strand of dark hair fall over his forehead, covering his left eye.

"Not as often as her and mostly non-fiction," she said, her eyes stuck to that strand of hair.

"What do you often do then?" he asked with curiosity shining through his callous-looking eyes.

"Work. And when I'm not working, I mostly go out and... do things."

She was still staring at his face.

The sunlight streaming in generously illuminated his features in a way that made her believe, just for a second, that the world was full of rainbows and unicorns for such a beautiful man to exist.

(In those seconds, she was fully deluding herself.)

His delicate features were now twisted into a deeply thoughtful look. "I see, I see. That was a brilliantly described answer. Very helpful. You have my thanks."

She blinked at his overly grave tone before letting out a laugh. "What I mean is, I like going on tiny adventures. Something to... make my life worth living, you know?"

His look was soft as if he truly understood her and the thought was scary enough to immediately make her want to provoke him.

"By the way, did you kill your father as the tabloids say?

... okay, that might have been a little too provoking. But it wasn't like she could take it back.

There was a storm in his eyes, unrelenting and unforgiving. He pursed his lips, as if to lie, and then, deciding otherwise, smoothed his expression back to friendliness.

"I did," he said, not offering further explanation. His tone, mild.

She knew she hit a significant spot. She filed that information away for later use.

Well, he now knew that she was aware of his identity. How he reacted to that would be vital to the future.

He turned away from her to look over the vista. His dark, long lashes fluttered along the soft breeze, almost touching the skin on his cheeks and dancing along with the light freckles.

"My mother loves reading romance like your friend, Selene. She likes the idea of happily ever after with your one true love."

So he didn't mind her knowing. The situation was under control then.

She looked at the bustling city below, standing side by side with him.

"You'd better call her Iclyn. She hates being called Selene almost as much as she hates vodka," she quickly told him.

Selene would start calling him unrefined or worse, crass if she heard him not address her by 'Iclyn' and thus have another reason to complain about him.

Blaise gave her an inquiring look and she knew what he was asking.

With a mischievous smile, she said, "I call her Selene because it gives my soul peace when I irritate her. And it's not like she's innocent either. She calls me Lilithe even though she knows how much it annoys me."

She then held up her hand. "But anyone else calling her Selene will be six feet under. Only I can get away with that."

"Looks like she cares for you a lot."

Lily's eyes widened and she quickly placed a finger on his soft-as-petals lips, silencing him effectively.

"Are you trying to curse me? Don't say such creepily foreshadowing words."

He blinked in confusion.

She was suddenly aware of how close she was to him, the pheromone of lavender soothing her senses. With their height difference, her eyes were right in front of his lips. Those exact lips where one of her fingers was currently placed.

Her craze-filled eyes trailed up to his unrelenting ones. Swirls of emotions, hard and cold, were displayed in his eyes. Try as she might, she couldn't detect desire, or anything close to it.

Lily was severely disappointed.

Eyes burning with rebellious intent, she reached out a finger to slowly push away the dark strand of hair from his eye.

The action didn't change his expression in the slightest. But his eyes calmly and intently studied her like a fascinating equation he was trying to solve. He seemed to really want the final value.

She didn't like that look.

Holding back the urge to say something even more provoking than before, she stepped away from him with an unaffected grin.

"Emotions, especially care and love, are a forbidden zone for Selene. So don't make the mistake of bringing it up, ever," she advised him. "Besides, she just lets me off because I helped her before. That's all."

He nodded in understanding though something told her he was a bit sceptical about the last part of her dialogue.

"By the way," he then lightly asked, changing the topic. "Will you allow me to join you on your tiny adventures next time?"

"If you're worthy of it, sure," she teased.

There we have the next meeting!

Some information on Selene was unfolded, what are your thoughts on it?

BTW, do any of you like reading non-fiction? I'm curious.

Chapter 7

<hr>

It had been a few minutes since she walked him out. It was a spontaneous decision - him arriving at her doorstep, he'd told her.

He had left after ever so politely requesting her to call him, so he can leave with her number on his phone. He had seemed a tad bit upset that she hadn't called even after basically extorting his number that night.

For someone who wasn't physically attracted to her, he seemed pretty attached, already. What was happening?

But then she shrugged off that thought.

Maybe her bountiful and endless charms couldn't help but make an impression on him.

That's just how she was.

Yep. That was the reason.

With confident strides, she breezed into the living room and sprawled down on the velvet sofa beside Selene who was almost at the end of her novel.

"So, what's this one about?" Lily asked.

"A queen in disguise ventures out of her palace and slowly falls for a carefree boy - not knowing that he's the number one outlaw in her city; the one who wants her dead." She then raised her head to lock her frosty blue eyes with Lily's forest green ones; face void of emotions. "Imagine what happened when they both found out the other's true identity."

Playing dumb, she said laughingly, "There's an explosion of emotions - messy and complicated - which they both overcome like they always do and then get married and live happily ever after with five kids?"

As Selene went back to reading without giving away any of her emotions, as usual, Lily thought that was the end of it.

Unfortunately not.

"This is a novel, Lilithe... this is a romance novel." Lily peered up in surprise as Selene spoke once again, her eyes trained on the book this time. "You don't know how real life will turn out, you can never predict that."

Her voice sounded as flat as was normal but on a closer look, Lily thought that maybe she could distinguish a smidgen of... melancholy.

But that wasn't possible.

What did Selene have to be melancholy about?

There wasn't a single living person she cared about. Because of her childhood, Selene grew up prioritizing material things and fictional people over real ones.

Lily had always been aware of that.

So she shrugged it off, once again.

Instead, she said, "Blaise told me that his mother likes reading romance just as you."

"He has a good relationship with his mother, it seems."

Lily paused for a second, searching Selene's face which, as always, betrayed nothing. "That's the feeling I got as well. He had this... affectionate look on his face when he was talking about her. But he admitted that he killed his father. But after spending time with him today, I'm more sure than ever, the rumours of why he killed the previous Boss are wrong."

"Maybe something related to his mother?"

Lily raised an arched brow. "Why would you say that?"

Selene's shoulder lifted a millimetre, imitating a shrug. "Just a feeling I got."

Lily rolled her eyes, smiling. "You and your feelings."

"That sounds wrong."

"Whatever."

"Lilithe."

"What now? Also, don't call me-"

"You just asked him whether he killed his father or not?"

Lily pursed her lips. "He was being too understanding about how I spend my time. It... didn't feel good."

Selene blinked a couple of times. Inclined her head to the side, studying her. She seemed genuinely surprised. "You told him the truth? You?"

... she did.

Lily didn't know why it just occurred to her. Maybe she was getting slow with age. But she was just twenty! That wasn't old!

Selene was older by two years, why did she catch on to it faster?

But it was true.

Lily realized as she replayed their whole conversation, she never once lied to him, never even entertained the thought of it.

Lily recalled what Selene had told her in the past:

"As expressive as you might seem, between the two of us, we both know you hide the most. Whatever little I say, I mean. Half of the things that come out of your mouth are lies."

Lily's smile had deepened. "I'm found out. Whatever will I do now?"

Looking at Selene now, Lily could understand why she was so surprised.

There was just something about Blaise...

He was deadly. She could see it in his cold-blooded eyes. Eyes which heated her blood - made her heart race faster. But at the same time, his expressions, and his manner of talking made her feel so at ease.

The feeling was addictive.

Maybe she was muddleheaded, unable to think straight over the adrenaline streaming through her blood vessels, but she shrugged it off again.

She'd just lie more next time.

Not a big deal.

Blaise entered his Bugatti and the driver started driving away from the obsidian skyscraper. He inspected his face through the side mirror and wondered what made Lilithe stare all the time with those eyes filled with madness.

Perhaps he was good looking but she must have seen better. There were loads of good-looking guys around the world.

He looked out the window and the wind flew past his face.

If there was one thing he was sure of after today, it was that she wasn't an ordinary person. That was the only way her reactions would make sense. Especially to his admittance of the previous Boss' murder.

But that didn't matter.

Whoever she was, was her own business. He was more interested in what made her rapidly ask that question in the first place with a daring look in her eyes.

She had opened up to him. Perhaps that made her anxious?

He was not sure.

The ferocious wind made a mess of his hair. Dark strands obstructed his vision. As he ran a hand through his wild locks, trying to organize them into a semblance of normalcy, he remembered how she had come closer to do something similar. He remembered the warm finger on his lips. The fragrance of Jasmine, sweet and sensual, had wafted to him.

This was the first time he had been so close to a woman.

Lilithe was fascinating. He didn't expect to enjoy her company so much.

He certainly didn't expect to want to get closer.

Blaise is starting to feel for a certain someone. (It's okay, Blaise, you can do it)

Hope you enjoyed this chapter!

Chapter 8

- -

Blaise called her the next day.

Lily didn't even try to suppress her smug and delighted smile. He was certainly enchanted, whether he liked it or not.

"Someone couldn't wait to hear my voice," she teased quite as soon as she picked up.

"Can you blame me? You have a voice that's passed down in legends," he said lightly, his own velvet voice worthy of being passed down.

"Why did you call? You could just come over like yesterday."

"I... did not want to creep you out." He sounded embarrassed.

After he already arrived yesterday? This man's logic was too twisted.

So she decided to embarrass him further. "Too late for that. I'm already super creeped out."

"You had my number but didn't call. I did not know what else to do."

His, equal parts embarrassed and defensive, tone made the corners of her lips turn up.

"Are you, maybe, trying to justify your creepiness? That's bad."

That clearly hit a strand of morality. "That isn't what I was doing. I know I am wrong so I did not want to further indulge in it."

Alright, she had enough fun at his expense.

"Chill, I'm kidding." She chuckled. "If I was creeped out even a bit, I would have made it very clear to you yesterday. Preferably by shoving you down the balcony."

"Violent." Yet, he sounded relieved. "But that's good to hear. I don't want to make you uncomfortable."

There he went again with the added mile of trying to make her feel at ease. Inexplicably.

"Why does the Boss of the Italian mafia care about my feelings so much?" Though her manner of asking seemed teasing, she was genuinely curious.

He seemed to pause for a moment, not sure of what he should say. His voice was soothing when he asked, "Why do you think?"

Through the glass window, Lily looked up into the cerulean sky, sifting through the fluffy strings of clouds as an almost overwhelmingly heavy feeling settled in the pit of her stomach - a feeling that had no business being there.

What she couldn't understand was his extra effort to ensure her comfort. But that he was bewitched and enraptured. That she was a sultry sight of untamed beauty - a fiery display of wilderness. That much she knew and understood.

It was nothing new.

Then a thought crept in, shaking her momentum. If that was the case, why did she see no speck of desire in his eyes at that moment? Why was he so infuriatingly unaffected?

The silence must have crackled on the other line for too long for he said, "The reason I called was to ask you about your next tiny adventure."

Brought out of her bubble of thought, she asked, "What do you want to know?"

"Can I join?"

"No."

"... You agreed to it last time."

"Did I? I remember saying: If you were worthy."

"Please?" His voice was gentle in a way that made Lily sure that this man was designed with the sole purpose of making her go muddleheaded.

A laugh escaped her; some parts helpless, some parts amused.

"Why on earth do you want to join? Don't you have money to make? People to kill? Besides, you don't even know what I'm going to do."

The background check, she was a hundred per cent sure, he did on her would have shown her record clean - courtesy of Selene, the Queen of Hacking.

Unless he tried to fit in all the minor details which led to him finding out the holes in her fake story. But men rarely invested that much effort.

So why would he?

"I want to spend more time with you. Is it a crime?"

"In that case, we can have dinner together. Let's go to that restaurant of yours where you took me last time."

Blaise Roosevelt never thought the day would come when he abandoned morals and all sense of decency to stalk a woman like a lecherous creep.

She was naturally flirtatious, he realised, he realized as he kept watching her interactions with men. It was nothing serious but he supposed she had the mentality of 'if offered, why refuse?'.

The thing was, her eyes danced with amusement all the time… and mocking laughter like she was only playing with them.

She was bold and brazen; she drew in everyone's gazes. She seemed drunk in the attention. She seemed to thrive.

It didn't take long before it occurred to Blaise that maybe she craved control. If she went through what he was sure she did go through, that would make perfect sense.

Which helpless victim didn't want to feel in control of their life, of themself again?

She was walking along the sidewalk when she encountered a girl, clad in rags, sitting in the corner. She stared down at her for a long time, ripples forming in her unhinged eyes. Snapping herself out of it soon, she kept on moving.

She went to a bar next.

It was the same bar where he first laid his eyes on her. He was still infuriated over the warehouse burning down and Lorenzo was his particular target for venting. His fury had grown tenfold when he saw that blackguard preying on an innocent woman.

Except, she turned out to be not so innocent.

(Not that it would've been any more acceptable if the woman being preyed on wasn't innocent.)

Lilithe was ordering and gulping down shots of wine like there was no tomorrow. She was particularly close to the bartender with wild, chestnut curls, sending him playful smiles and receiving his dimpled ones in return.

When a man who had been eyeing her for the past ten minutes came beside her seat with a suggestive smile, she took his hand, flashing him a smirk, and pulled him to the dance floor.

She danced with her dark hair flying, wild and alluring, along the tempo. Her olive skin glowed and her smile curled men's toes. The man she was against was drunk in her rather than the wine as if all his hopes and dreams were realized.

But when Blaise took a clear look at her eyes, he didn't trust the rascally glint in them.

She looked drunk but he knew she wasn't.

They were around people who were wasted and busy moving their bodies in sync with the blaring music. But she was pretending. And because he was watching intently, he saw her hands creep down that man's pocket and skillfully slide out his wallet.

After getting what she wanted, she promptly disappeared from his arms, entering another set of arms, then another, until she successfully made him dizzy and tired of looking for her.

But Blaise wasn't tired. He watched the entire debacle with rapture till the end.

She wasn't an innocent woman like he had thought when he first saw her, but Blaise didn't mind.

The air outside was refreshing and cool. Untainted by the stench of sweaty bodies inside.

Blaise didn't like bars and their oppressive cacophony.

His eyes were still tracking the reason for his entrance at that place. She was walking away with confidant strides, flipping her thick curls over her shoulder without any sign of anxiety.

With the ease she was exuding, it must be a normal occurrence for her.

Taking out the wallet, she brought out the thick wad of cash from inside. It would seem she deliberately targeted a rich man.

Blaise followed her to that girl by the street.

Lilithe bent down to grab her arms and successfully pulled her up from her position on the ground. She placed the cash in her hand while asking, "It's late at night. Are you foolish?"

The girl down looked at the money and then up at her. She opened her mouth but Lily turned away without hearing her out.

Towards the park.

At this time of the night, the park was more or less isolated.

He entered through the gates, staring at the woman who sat on one of the benches, staring up at the blanket of glittering stars above.

As he went closer, she spoke up amidst the silence, "Why are the stars so bright today? And why is the moon so shameless? It dares to shine so vividly after having stolen someone else's light."

Blaise was silent.

"What's wrong? Won't talk after following me all day long?"

She turned her head to face him. The moonlight cast on her face made it seem luminous. Her forest green eyes glistened like emeralds, beckoning him closer and closer...

He closed his eyes, breathing in and out steadily. When he finally opened them, he found her lips curled with a knowing look in those eyes.

"If you were planning on joining me regardless of my wish, why did you bother asking me in the first place?"

She was right, of course. What he did tonight was out of line. She didn't want him to join but he went against her wishes.

He felt bad about it.

But how would he get to know more about her if he did not join her in doing things that she liked to do?

Of course, that didn't excuse his actions. He knew it. His only consolation was that she didn't look unhappy or violated because of him. Quite the contrary, in fact.

So he asked lightly, "This is your fun adventure, then?"

Her smile stretched to a smirk. "One of many types."

"But you gave the money to that girl." He wasn't trying to insult her or anything but she never really seemed the kind and generous type.

"Why not?" She shrugged, uncaring. "I don't need the money."

"But you did that-"

"Because it's fun." She was smiling at him with sparkling eyes. "Isn't it so thrilling when you know that you might get caught, but you might not if you're skilled enough, which I am? Doesn't it just electrify you when you get the chance to play with fire?"

Blaise tried hard to understand the thrill of danger, but he couldn't. He was in danger along with his mother his whole life. He had no wish to go through that again.

Lilithe chuckled, looking at his face, as she stood up from her seat and took several deliberate steps towards him. "It's alright if you can't understand. All you need to know is that I love playing with fire, so you should just stand still and let me."

She was close to him again. This time, the smell of wine drifted to him along with Jasmine.

The madness within her eyes that had been brewing for years, richer than decades-old wine, lured him in.

His breathing was shaky. His heart raced miles per minute. He clenched his trembling fists and wondered if it was delayed tiredness from walking after her so long.

She talked of playing with fire but in his eyes, she was the fire. Much as she tried to hide it, he knew she burned inside. And for the first time in his life, he wanted to get closer.

In the end, if he turned to ashes, he would let the wind guide him to her.

Is that love I smell? Took him long enough!

Also, Blaise is such a stalker. His mother would be very disappointed.

Chapter 9

He walked her home.

He was initially going to give her a ride but she had insisted on sobering up from the cool air.

As if she needed it.

Her alcohol tolerance was high. She'd just wanted to walk with him on a starry night.

Throughout the whole walk, he seemed a bit off as if he had, just now, made an earth-shattering revelation. As if something hit him like a heavy ton of bricks.

A far cry from his usual calm and composed self.

Given his reactions - from the light widening of his mahogany eyes to the guileless fluttering of his dark long lashes - whenever she got close to him, she'd think he had never been close to a woman before.

Did she spook him somehow?

By the time they reached her building, Lily was left with question upon question.

As she gave him a parting smile before entering, she could have sworn there was a hint of rosy patches nestled on his cheeks. But they were gone before she could fixate on them, leaving her questioning whether they really were present.

But given the disturbance among the callousness that floated in his eyes back in the park, Lily was confident he was no longer as unaffected as he had been in the past.

So she chose to be optimistic.

Entering her room, the first place she strode to was the bathroom. After a long day, submerging herself in lukewarm water was extremely rewarding. She usually liked to use jasmine-scented bath bombs but this time she chose lavender.

Crazy how much it relaxed her muscles and calmed her mind.

Lily thought she was going to die, or at least, get very close to it when she first spotted him following her. But if she reacted too strongly, that might make him suspicious. So she pretended to not notice it and then acted like it didn't matter.

His eyes pierced through her the whole time in that bar. She could feel his gaze on her when she was dancing with her target for the night. For one inexplicable second, she feared he might interrupt them and mess up her plan.

It had happened before.

Men tended to be possessive of her whenever she was dating them. She didn't like it. But changing her boyfriends like clothes didn't help much - all were the same.

While she always firmly made her boundaries clear, she didn't take any serious steps because she never dated any of them long enough for it to create any major conflict.

Maybe she couldn't understand their emotions properly. That didn't matter. She couldn't properly explain it but whenever it happened, she felt restricted and suffocated.

She had spent seven years of her life feeling that way, and another four years trying not to feel that way.

Was she wrong for being utterly tired of it?

No, she wasn't.

And she didn't care if she was.

She was only pleasantly surprised when Blaise was just carefully watching her.

And she liked it.

She had decided to let him off easy for stalking her after that.

When he had asked her why she gave the money to that homeless girl, she had entertained the thought of lying and telling him it was just her wanting to help the poor and the needy. That looking towards the girl tugged at her heartstrings.

Her mind had flashed back to that girl, awfully skinny with no shine in her eyes. For a moment, Lily had the thought of time travel being possible for that girl had reminded her of herself, under the care of her so-called uncle. He and his depraved followers had torn down a girl's earnest trust and shattered her innocence - splintering it into a million scattered pieces.

Pity, they didn't watch out for how sharp the broken edges were.

Being faced with such a vision, how could she walk away?

Lily had thought of the helpless little girl she had been, with no one by her side willing to offer a hand. Fighting the feeling of meeting her past self, she wanted to help this girl at present when no one else did. Sitting at the streetside, at that time of the night, who knew what could've happened to her? What sort of men she'd have caught the eyes of? By doing this, if there was a chance of Lily diverting such a fate from the future of another girl, Lily had believed it wouldn't be a waste of her time.

Obviously, she couldn't tell Blaise all that. But the lovely lies which, otherwise, smoothly sailed off her tongue did not come out. She had settled for a half-truth.

After all, she really did not need more money.

They frequently talked, over the phone or face to face, the next few days. She always invited him whenever she wanted to set things on fire, or con someone.

He'd follow her anyway so she felt her calling him was a better choice.

She wasn't sure if she'd like it since she had never included her previous boyfriends in her plans. But she was unexpectedly rejoicing in this.

Blaise could fade into the background and let her do her thing.

He wasn't loud or aggressive, and neither did he find the need to exert dominance or whatever it was men with fragile egos did.

With him, she never felt threatened. Her authority, her power and control never felt threatened. He was quiet and mild and he always went along with her.

After making plans over text, Lily turned off her phone and went in search of Selene.

She was perched on the light velvet sofa with a disturbed aura. Her lower lip jutted out the tiniest bit while her chubby cheeks were a little puffed. A snowy blizzard was happening in her eyes - looking at them would give a person shivers.

"What's wrong?" Lily asked in surprise. "Who bullied you?"

Selene slowly glanced at her with a withering look. "Maybe I bullied them, instead."

Her tone was monotonous as always and her features smoothed back into expressionless.

Lily didn't press further. Selene would tell her of her own accord when she was ready to.

She went to the topic she was going to talk to her about. Days with Blaise were a treat but she couldn't forget her main purpose.

"I wanted to ask you to work on Alfonzo next. You need to be extra careful this time. Santano must be pissed because I burned his warehouse. He lost a lot of money."

"Santano is the next one."

Yes, he was. After two years, her revenge will reach completion.

Anticipation caked her thoughts and her lips hooked in a serpentine smile.

"How I will enjoy his fearful expression when I finally get to him. He will see how it feels to slowly tear down a person's shields step by step, leaving them for last." Lily peered at Selene with eyes full of wrath and madness. "I hope he trembles, Selene. I hope he falls on his knees and begs me... like he made me do continuously for seven freaking years."

Selene's eyes were the coldest winter. "I will have to hack the CCTV system so I can watch it live."

And she knew. Lily knew Selene was going to stay with her till the end.

I'm not the fondest of this chapter. My writing definitely took a turn for the worst here.

On the brighter side, we're going to be watching Lily terrorizing another person, soon! Just you wait, Alfonzo...

BTW, what are your thoughts on our main couple's progression?

Chapter 10

Weeks passed by quickly.

Lily knew Selene was working hard on getting to Alfonzo. But she also knew that whatever had bothered her, it kept growing worse.

She was in an awfully bad mood these days.

So Lily steered clear of her. Who knew, Selene might get mad for real and stop helping her.

It was boring not being able to annoy her though. It was, after all, her much-cherished habit.

When Selene went out to have lunch with her latest victi-ahem-lover, Lily was very much relieved.

Maybe her black mood will drop down.

She always came back particularly pleased after a fresh murder.

Selene might have features that conveyed an innocence, worthy of being preserved yet nobody except Lily knew that woman was worse than a succubus.

Given how every man involved with her ended up dead, Selene was a prime example of why one shouldn't judge people based on their appearances.

Guess why they ended up dead, though?

Well, she killed them!

They caught her eye, poor unfortunate souls they were, and she caught theirs. They went on dates and she went to their place for the night. The following day, the sun rose but those men didn't.

Selene never liked feeling. She never liked the fluttering of her heart, the warmth spreading throughout her body or the heady desire hitching her breath.

Lily remembered the first time she did it.

Her small porcelain hands had been dripping with blood. The crimson blood, particularly eye-catching staining the fair skin. There was a quark of satisfaction swimming in those cold, indifferent eyes.

"I did it. I killed it," she had murmured flatly. Looking up at her in triumph, she'd revealed, "I surpassed my-that woman."

But was it really surpassing if she did exactly what that woman had been teaching her to do? Wasn't that playing right into her hands? But Lily didn't want to alienate her.

So she had kept quiet.

Even as she knew the point wasn't that she killed a man, Lily couldn't care less what happened to him, but that Selene had cut off the roots to certain emotions before they could dare to think of being bright in bloom.

But living such a life, how was it different to not living at all? Maybe this was why Selene was always immersed in the world of romance. She wouldn't have it, any of it, in real life.

Maybe this was why Selene often talked with her about the moments of friendships between the phantom characters on the yellowed pages of books. She wouldn't allow herself to acknowledge the friendship she had for real. But Lily didn't mind. She wasn't very well-versed in sentimental talks either.

But let alone love, even something as trivial as physical attraction was enough to disturb Selene to the point of those men having their throats slit - thanks to the woman by their bedside. After all, there was always the potential for it to grow into more.

Was it a completely normal and morally right thing to do?

No.

But Lily couldn't be bothered to care about such minor details. Just a few men. The world was overpopulated, anyway.

She took steps guiding her to the balcony overlooking the city. When her phone rang, Lily was surprised to see it was Selene but picked up nonetheless.

"Join me for lunch... my date ran away."

Say what now?

"I do not know what's wrong. Recently, everyone I have been targe-attracted to runs away... like they know how they're all going to end up." Selene looked down at her food, picking on her salad.

She looked ethereal, her silver hair streaming down like a waterfall and her soft pink dress. The play of light from the windows nearby only gave her the aura of an otherworldly creature.

On the other hand, Lily had rushed in here when Selene called. She was considerably messier looking, not as poised and elegant.

"I mean..." Lily started in reply, holding back the chortle. "Running away is kind of the normal thing to do when you know that you're going to be killed."

"Something bizarre is going on. Does anyone know? But I always thoroughly clean up my traces."

Lily understood this was the cause of her atrocious mood these days.

"How many has it been?"

"Four."

"Four murders you couldn't commit. Unacceptable."

Her teasing didn't help. Selene started picking on her salad more aggressively.

"Easy there." Lily stopped her delicate-looking hand - who would've guessed it was so strong? "The poor salad didn't do anything. It deserves to be eaten with relish. Now, tell me what you think must have gone wrong."

"I do not know. They are not scared or hesitant when we first meet. And they even come to our designated date spot but something happens during that time and instead of getting out of their car, they speed back away. As if they are seeing an unknown entity instead of me."

"Why didn't you chase after them to ask?" That was the most logical thing to do, right? Demand an explanation for being stood up?

Her eyes turned frostier as if she was extremely offended. "Why would I do such a disgraceful thing?"

Lily sighed, helplessly. Of course.

It was that damn pride.

Lily sighed some more in resignation.

"Alright, then. Next time, send me your date's address. I'll chase him for you. We'll get answers then. Hopefully."

"No," came the succinct reply. "I am done with my dates running away. I will just kidnap them next time."

Lily blinked, too astounded to speak. Don't get her wrong, Lily was quite self-aware. She knew her brain had a few loose screws. But she seemed to lose that race when Selene existed.

She looked around the restaurant, the different couples having lunch around them, until something caught her eye. "By the way, Selene, that waiter's been eyeing you."

"Not interested."

"Your dates keep ghosting you, how come you're still so picky?"

But Selene ignored her, calmly drinking her glass of sparkling water.

Whatever.

After she was done eating, Lily took her phone to text Blaise. She wanted to shop around but Selene was in no mood to join her.

Besides, she needed someone to carry her bags.

So... huh. What's your opinion on Selene now?

And we saw a different side of their friendship; one where Lily isn't annoy-ing her for the fun of it.

Chapter 11

Blaise got the text when he was done having lunch with his mother.

His phone gave a soft ping. And the lock screen showed the name Lilithe.

He and his mother were sitting side by side, leading her hawk-like eyes to immediately glance at the ostentatious flashing of the name. A resulting smile bloomed on her face.

"Are you two getting closer?"

Blaise read through the text and said, "She is getting more comfortable with me, it would seem. I am glad."

This way, it might not be long before she opened up to him.

"How exactly did you want to help her?" his mother asked.

Blaise hesitated, pondering. "I did not think that far in the beginning. I want to get justice for her, I suppose. Punish those who turned her life into a nightmare."

She hid so much.

She thought he did not see it but he did. He saw right through her because he knew what to look for. Because he had seen it before.

A life full of cynicism and mistrust. How exhausting must it be to not believe?

Shaking off his heavy thoughts, he glanced at his mother. "She asked me to join her for shopping."

His mother's almond eyes widened and she stood up at lightning speed. The chair she was sitting on slid away, making a rough noise against the marble floor. "Like a date?"

"Not really." Blaise ruthlessly dumped a pitcher of cold water on her. "More like she needs someone to-"

"What are you even waiting for? Quickly go."

He was promptly kicked out of his own mansion, the door slammed in his face.

Disbelief clouding his features, he stared at the closed door.

Seconds passed and with that, followed an eternity, yet the door remained heartlessly shut. Therefore, he got in his car and drove to where he was actually wanted.

She strode out of the restaurant, confidence streaming out with every bounce of her dark curls, as soon as she spotted him through the glass walls. A delighted smile etched at the corner of her surprisingly not-red lips. Thinking of it, she did not look as carefully dressed up as she almost always was when outside.

"Yes, yes," she said, following his gaze. "I went out in a hurry today so didn't have time to get ready."

He raised an eyebrow deliberately letting surprise rush through his eyes. "This is you not having time to get ready? The rest of us might as well stop existing."

All these years of flattering his mother made him quite an expert in the art of sweet talk full of honeyed words.

"I know right? I'm just too stunning." She played along with mischief flashing in her eyes.

"Absolutely gorgeous."

It was her turn to raise eyebrows at those two words. "You've been holding that in for a long time, haven't you?

He shrugged nonchalantly, moving away and leading her to his car.

She swiftly got in after he opened the door for her. And so, for the next five hours, he kept driving her to different shopping complexes and his car was flooded with bags and bags full of clothes and jewellery.

"I wish I had two heads." That weird sentence came out of her as she was mournfully looking at all the necklaces on display.

"Two heads will not do," he told her. "You'd have to be a hydra."

"I'd be a pretty hydra, no?" She smirked.

"Why, of course. You are always pretty."

When they went to the cosmetics store, that was when he was truly tried.

"Which shade of red lipstick do you think will suit me best? I usually go with scarlet since it's the perfect balance of orange and red. But I should try out another shade, right?"

He picked up the one closest to him and showed her. "What about this?"

Her eyes widened in horror, looking at him like he was a villain. Well, he sort of was, but he didn't expect her to view him this way because of lipstick.

"Not Fuchsia. That would dull out my glowing complexion. Anything with a cool undertone wouldn't suit me. Mine must be yellow or orange based since I have a warm undertone. Besides, this one has terrible pigmentation."

He dutifully nodded his head at all the right times pretending to have even the slightest idea of what she was talking about.

The saleswoman in front of them apparently did, for she presented a few different shades to her which she didn't immediately reject in alarm as she did with his suggestion.

"Coral or poppy? Both suit me."

She still wanted him to comment?

Blaise very seriously scrutinised the two shades of red lipstick. But try as he might, he could not see the difference between these two. Perhaps he needed to check in with an ophthalmologist?

"Well..." he trailed off helplessly and looked back at her, blinking.

"You don't even see the difference, do you?" She sighed.

Something about the resignation in sigh as the words 'men' seemed to float in her eyes offended him immensely.

"I do see the difference. This one is... so and so and that one... is a little different."

Her eyebrows raised up, unimpressed.

He continued without fail, "Overall, you will be a dazzling vision in both so you should not limit yourself to just choosing one of them. Why don't you buy both?"

His face warmed once he was done talking. Not only her, he could feel the saleswoman's gaze on him as well. He turned himself away and strode out of the store, towards his car. The light breeze cooled his heated cheeks and his clenched fists relaxed.

She followed him soon after.

Resolutely not giving her a glance, he opened the car door and stood aside, waiting for her to get in. He felt her eyes on him; she wasn't getting in but the recent embarrassment fresh in his mind, he tried to keep his cool.

He looked towards her, tilting his head. "What is it?"

She was still staring.

With a teasing curl to her lips, she said, "You look extra gorgeous when you're flustered."

It took everything he had to stop the blood from flowing to his cheeks once again. It was unbelievable how difficult controlling his emotions became ever since he met this woman.

She could have him blushing like a school kid with just a smile.

Ignoring how his heart fluttered, ready to yield to her will, he took the last few bags from her and put them in the car.

At this rate, there'd be no space for the two of them in there.

Blaise thought when all the space was used up, Lilithe would stop but no. She then asked for home delivery.

... why not do that from the beginning?

"Because having the physical evidence of the things I've brought right beside me gives me a feeling of satisfaction."

Also, was she even going to wear half of the things she bought? He did not think she would finish wearing all of them in a lifetime.

"Are you a woman or am I a woman?"

Blaise wisely shut up after that.

As the sky darkened with the setting of the sun, her shopping spree was finally over. She entered the cramped car, ogling at the items.

He was about to release a sigh of relief when he spotted her eyes sparkling with delight as she looked through some of the things she bought.

Never mind, maybe he should ask her to go shopping more often. He would bring a more spacious car next time.

On that note, he was also going to study the different shades of red so he did not disappoint her next time.

Looks like Blaise's mom is a staunch supporter of their relationship XD

Also, Lily's attitude when shopping is what I wish I could be like! But I'm too poor for that.

Chapter 12

After the shopping spree, he took her to a restaurant for dinner. The one where they dined on their first meeting.

Sure enough, the staff members blanched once they took note of him.

That same middle-aged guy from earlier stepped in.

"A private room, as per usual, sir?"

"As per usual."

It was a sleek and sophisticated private room on the upper floor. The walls were painted in a cool gray, creating a contrast with the dark wood floor. The windows were covered with sheer curtains, letting the occupants bask in the silvery light.

Lily looked at the chairs surrounding the table, upholstered with black leather and chrome legs, and wondered out loud:

"Why didn't you go with this one last time?"

"I did not want you to feel uncomfortable being alone with a strange man, especially after what you went through." His eyes bore into her, relentless and intense, as he calmly pulled the chair back for her.

A thought made intruded at the front of her mind, increasing the palpitations of her heart, what did he know?

But she shrugged off the budding unease, escaping once again, as she sat down on the chair pulled back for her, draping one leg over the other. "So now you don't think I'll be uncomfortable anymore?"

"Would it be too bold of me to assume we are friends, now?"

"Friends?" She laughed. "We're no longer strangers, I'll give you that much."

"Ouch." He had a carefree smile on his face. "Whatever will I have to do to reach that level, then?"

He sat himself down across from her, face tilted indolently to the side.

She leaned towards him with a look in her eyes that was no less than tantalizing. "You want to be friends with me, Blaise?"

Blaise seemed to be at a loss for a few moments before he replied, leaning towards her as well, "And if you will allow it, maybe something more."

His gaze was all-consuming, emotions swirling like a cyclone. She recognized the ever-present callousness in his eyes, those were nothing new. She discovered the hidden desire reserved for her. But she couldn't guess at that one specific emotion that was slowly overtaking all else, a bit more every time she met him.

What was it?

It was alarming as much as it was unfamiliar.

Lily didn't want to overthink. She didn't want to ruin anything.

So Lily did what she was good at. She leaned back, pretending that moment didn't happen.

"You mean, you want us to date?" She asked him instead in a laughing manner.

Something close to forbearance passed through his eyes, in a way that softened its callus edges. His soft lips hooked in a blithe smile. "Is it funny? Am I to be laughed at for liking you?"

"I wasn't laughing at that. It's just that..." she defended herself, eyes twinkling, as she rapidly thought up a reason. "You often talk like you're in the medieval era or something."

A mesmeric chuckle sounded. "I guess reading so many classics growing up stuck with me."

"You like reading?"

"You sound surprised."

"Well... I mean-" A lean finger pressed against her lips, making her swallow back the next words.

"Have mercy, Queen Lilithe. This humble peasant cannot bear your harsh disdain."

She wanted to say many things to him in reply. She wanted to praise him for knowing exactly what to say. She wanted to tell him to call her Lily. She wanted to finish her words of 'harsh disdain'.

But her lips were currently being restrained. And talking would require freeing them. Yet, this was the kind of restraint she would happily undergo.

So she stared at him expectantly.

He was free to translate it to her being expectant for... anything really. It could be anything.

He leaned over the table towards her. She leaned in as well like she was hypnotized, close enough to count the light freckles over his nose bridge.

They looked so adorable, contrasting with his fair skin.

His finger on her lips slowly pulled away. Emptiness followed and she pursed her lips.

A lock of her hair swung forward and his fingers latched on it. Reaching out, he hooked it behind her ear, fingers grazing the delicate lobe of her ear, down her neck before landing on her shoulder in a solid, yet unspeakably gentle grip.

"Remember when you did something similar to me back at your home? I saw the disappointment in your eyes, then." His voice was a whisper that sent shivers through her body, doubling her heartbeat. With each breath she took, she took in more of his fragrance. That scent of lavender which calmed and soothed her like nothing ever managed to. "Why were you disappointed, Lily?"

She remembered.

How could she not remember?

She reached out her own finger, grazing his skin, from the smoothness of his forehead to the softness of his cheek. Caressing his cheeks, she gave him an elusive smile. "Blaise, Blaise..."

His breath hitched. Dark long lashes fluttered tantalizingly against his snowy skin. Yet, his mahogany eyes were a clifftop - one she quickly realised she'd topple down from if she wasn't careful enough. Who knew if there'd be sharp rocks or a soft grassland below?

"All you need to know is that I'm no longer disappointed."

A knock on the door snapped them out of the tempting haze.

His hand on her shoulder gently ran down her arm as her hand on his cheek ran down his arm. Their hands were interlinked as the waiter arrived to take their order.

Just like the last time, he waited for her to give her order and choose the same things she did.

She raised a questioning eyebrow at him once they were alone again. "Why'd you choose the same items as me?"

He looked around helplessly. "Am I not allowed to?"

"You did the same previously."

"Maybe I just like the dishes you order since you have such excellent taste," he suggested with an amused smile.

She kept staring at him, unmoving.

He sighed. "Just because."

She blinked in confusion.

"I just wanted to eat the same types of food you did. There's no specific reason."

"Ah..." Lily tried to look like she got his reasoning. "That's..."

Stupid.

But she didn't say that out loud because she didn't want to hurt his feelings.

She was a lovely and considerate person and all that.

Blaise had a knowing smile on his face. "You think it is stupid, don't you?"

"You got me," she said, shrugging shamelessly.

He let out a soft laugh, not offended in the slightest.

"Speaking of, I'm so hungry," she complained. "Why isn't the food still here?"

"... It has only been two minutes, Lily."

Blaze turned on the Wall TV to stop her complaining

and offered her the remote. She gleefully accepted it, shuffling through the channels.

One channel, however, showed the news reporters discussing the Giovanni Family. As corrupt as they were, the public didn't know of the drug dealing its Capo was involved with. In the eyes of the media, Santano Giovanni was an honest businessman whose men were getting killed by a villainous culprit who they named: Ruby Wraith.

While the playful smile never left her lips, her eyes gradually turned hard.

But then their food arrived and she recollected herself, passing on to the next channel.

If Lily had known what would happen the following weeks because of her few moments of unwitting carelessness, she would have paid more care to the pair of sharp mahogany eyes that gradually turned cold.

So what do you think of that ending?! Originally, this chapter had a bit more but then I felt this would be a good time to end it.

So there you have it!

Chapter 13

After an enjoyable dinner, they both step out into the night's chill. Looking up at the dark canvas, it had uncountable drops of white sprinkled all over, glowing and lighting up the night.

Today's night sky was particularly bright. It was guiding all those who had no light.

She stared up, with vengeance in her wild eyes.

"You keep glaring at the stars." The light whisper at her ear surprised her.

"I just don't like how they shine so bright." She turned her head, eyes of forest green locking with mahogany - the distance between them, they were no more than a whisper away.

Her eyes trailed down to his rosy lips. She brought up her hand and her thumb gently stroked his lower lip. Eyes running up his face, contacting his, she hesitated.

She had never hesitated with anyone before.

Noticing her hesitation, his cold-blooded eyes melted. Melted in a way the precipice of a thousand pitfalls was washed off and in its place was a presence as caring as it was sincere.

He gently removed her thumb from his lips and took a step back.

Unknowingly, so did she.

When she saw his molten mahogany eyes, she found they were shiver-inducing but not quite the same way.

That scared her enough to consider running away.

(Wasn't that what she always did?)

She looked away, scanning the area as best as she could in her state of panic. The night was brightly lit. She wouldn't have much trouble running away.

But he wouldn't have a problem chasing after her either. He had a car but she didn't. She-

"Lilithe." The voice broke through her haze.

She released a pain-filled breath and looked back into his eyes.

And blinked in confusion.

He was looking at her with faint concern in his ruthless mahogany eyes. The tempest in that pair, as unrestrained as always.

Not even a little softness to them.

Was she seeing things now?

Her body, coiled to spring away at the slightest signal, gradually settled down. Her heart beat at a normal pace. And she slowly got back at ease.

She was calm throughout the whole drive. She didn't feel like running away again. She didn't freak out again.

Blaise glanced at her a couple of times through the rear-view mirror. She smiled at him each time, looking very carefree.

He didn't probe.

Wise guy.

But now that Lily was in control on again of her faculties, she was no longer unbalanced at the edge of uncertainty. Blaise was completely his usual self. That gentleness and care were only something she dreamed up. Her mind was playing tricks on her.

That was all.

Back to her playful self, she gave him a teasing look when they arrived at her building as he was going up the floors with her.

He blinked, scandalised.

But before he could come up with a piece to defend his honour, the sleek black door opened.

And Selene was standing right in front of them, staring at him.

Lily raised an eyebrow at her in intrigue. While Blaise, faced with Selene's icy gaze, didn't seem to know what to say.

As if he was afraid of saying the wrong thing and offending her.

"I apologize for arriving with her so late." He finally decided on it.

"Lilithe can come home whenever she wants to."

"Yes, of course," he amicably agreed. "I apologize if I insinuated anything else."

Lily was having the time of her life watching those two. Selene was trying to poke him and see his condition so far, while Blaise was doing everything he could to avoid offending her.

However, as Selene kept staring at him indifferently, lowering the temperature by a hundred or so degrees, Lily felt like she had to intervene before Blaise got frostbite.

"Okay, you two, it's late now. Blaise, thanks for coming up with me. I think the men downstairs are done bringing out all the bags from your car."

He nodded and after exchanging goodbyes, left.

The door closed with Selene and her inside the penthouse.

Selene did not glance at her. Instead, she seemed to be thinking deeply about something, comparing the pros and cons.

Lily was about to leave for her room when Selene spoke up, cool eyes fixed on the closed door:

"You still think everything is going perfectly under control?"

Lily cocked her head to the side. "What are you on about?"

Selene slowly turned around and faced her, ice blue clashing with forest green. Her face was void of emotions, yet the words she uttered next had her blood chilling.

"The look in his eyes, as he stared at you, did not seem casual, Lilithe. It seemed like a man who knew too much - one who was desperately drowning in love."

This chapter was a bit short. Since this was the next part of the previous chapter.

Also... Poor Blaise got his feelings exposed. For someone who barely shows any emotions, Selene sure is an expert at reading them.

But how's Lily going to react?! I'll give you a clue. It won't be pleasant.

Chapter 14

Selene had, thanks to her late mother, an impressive amount of assets in her name.

But she would never be bothered to care for them - Selene was the type who wanted to get something in return for nothing. She was only interested in enjoying luxuries, reading novels and - whenever she was in a restless mood - hacking into weird places.

Really weird places.

Lily, on the other hand, liked managing everything and just, being active instead of lazing around. Thus, she was the one willingly running Selene's business.

At the end of the day, the overall profit was split between the two.

Win-win situation, in her eyes.

Every few days, she would be at her office, finishing up her tasks and looking over all her employees. Except, she couldn't concentrate on her work properly this time around.

And that was infuriating because she loved doing things, anything, so long as she called the shots - which she did.

Instead of working on the paperwork, she had blanked out. Her secretary, Cora Lyriam, had to call her multiple times before she snapped out of her daze.

"Miss Blackthorne, you have been working hard these days... maybe you need some time off?" Cora had gently suggested.

"This is the first time I came to the office since five days ago," Lily had replied dryly.

Cora had hesitated.

"Is there, maybe, something on your mind? Anything I can help with?"

Of course not.

Lily had shrugged. "Maybe I just need to loosen up some."

And that's what brought her to the nightclub - Seraphine

It was an exclusive members-only club that she owned. More specifically, it was gifted to her by Selene.

In her words: "You are more into these messy and rowdy places than I am."

But this club wasn't messy! Selene was just prejudiced.

She entered the nightclub wearing a wine-coloured bodycon dress with a short leather jacket on top. The clicking of her stilettos over the marble floor was drowned out by the beat of the music.

Sitting down once inside, she took off the black jacket.

Looking around at everyone, truly in bliss, she had half a hope of loosening the knot of unease that had been building in her with increasing momentum.

Her eyes locked with a guy making his way to her, offering a drink which she accepted with a slow, practised smile. She took small, measured sips of the wine, keeping her provoking eyes on him.

He had brown eyes. That was the first thing she noticed. A mop of dark hair and fair skin.

A smirk was playing on his pink lips.

Her hand on the crystal glass tightened.

His eyes were on her as he led her to the dance floor. His gaze held the fire she used to like. But her smile directed at him wasn't genuine.

She didn't know why the strange feeling of wistfulness invaded her senses all of a sudden.

They danced in sync but her limbs felt robotic. Her arms snaked around his neck, her eyes locked to his.

Why did she wish for the calming mahogany instead of the dull brown?

His mischievous eyes promised a good time.

But why wasn't there ruthlessness in them?

He leaned his head towards her and she had to stop herself from searching for the freckles that weren't dotted over his nose. She wouldn't be able to count them. Because they weren't there.

"Want to go somewhere quieter?" He asked with a cocky smirk.

Lily had never seen him smirk.

Pushing away the guy, she stepped back from the dance floor. "Thanks for the offer, but I'd have to decline."

She sent him her own smirk so as to not seem as shaken as she felt at that moment. The music in her club had never seemed so oppressive. Surrounded by so many people, she had never felt so lonely.

Her phone rang and it was the same man who refused to leave her thoughts.

She ignored the call and texted him:

I'm busy. Don't bother me for the time being.

It was when the sun had started setting, the sky being a wondrous shade of scarlet, that Lily found herself taking simple steps towards the villa ahead.

The time had come for Alfonzo.

He had taken a weekend vacation with his mistress, while his wife was at home looking after her months-old child.

Which was just fine for Lily.

It was way easier sneaking into his vacation villa than his mansion. The security was less tight, for one. And the place was also in an isolated area - near the dense forest.

The cameras around had long been made useless by Selene and the drugs seeped into the food had immobilized the bodyguards.

It was almost pathetic.

Once inside, she watched out for the woman inside the house with him. She would have no choice but to kill the woman if she saw her face. It would be better if she could knock her unconscious before that can happen.

She readjusted the mask on her face.

As she neared the bedroom, she could hear noises inside. Needless to say, she wasn't going to open that door any time soon.

She got out a small piece of silk sprayed with knockout drugs.

She walked around a few paces before the disgusting noise seemed to subside from inside that room.

A relieved breath escaped her.

Her sharp hearing picked up the nimble footsteps nearing the door before the doorknob twisted. Lily tiptoed into the place where she would be behind the door once opened.

As the door opened and out came a brunette, Lily flew from her position and pressed the silk cloth on her face. There was a few moments of struggle, and muffled screams, before the feminine body gradually went limp.

The woman barely weighed anything to Lily as she steadily carried her on her back and deposited her in another room, at the other end of the villa.

She found a pen and tore a piece of paper from a notebook on the nearby desk and wrote:

Don't be worried. Just chill in here for a while. You'll be released soon.

She really hoped the woman listened to her advice and stayed put. Since these mafia men were quite infamous when it came to, uh, rumpling the sheets with countless ladies, this wasn't the first time Lily had to keep women locked up somewhere while she took care of the lechers.

She had met quite a few who

listened and stayed calm but then again, there were always those overtaken with panic and kept sobbing.

Lily could understand the panic due to not believing in measly notes of reassurance, it might just as easily be a lie, but that didn't mean it wasn't annoying as heck.

Lily then braced herself.

It was time to meet her next victim.

Lily's avoiding Blaise but how long can she avoid acknowledging her feelings? She's a stubborn one, I'm afraid, so it might be pretty long.

Also, you get another Lily-torturing-scumbags scene next chapter! Let me tell you, writing them feels quite cathartic.

Chapter 15

Lily arrived in steady steps at the door of the room that guy was in. As she turned the knob and entered, she heard his creepy drawl:

"Back already? Must be eager for round two."

"Round two, three, four... I could go on a torture rampage for hours if you'd let me," she replied in a bright voice, taking her mask off and putting it in her blazer pocket.

Alfonzo whipped his head towards her so fast she was shocked it didn't break off. His eyes trailed her red-clad figure, the cruel glint in her eyes and then realization sank in.

"Honestly, you men don't learn. Why would you isolate yourself with a vacation, lowering the security around you when your two members died not so long ago? You're that tired of your wife so you'd rather choose death?" But then she shrugged and handed him a smirk. "Not that I'm complaining, mind you. It only makes things easier for me."

"My men will come soon." He put on a brave expression. "The alarm system went off the moment you entered."

"The alarm system?" She blinked innocently. "Ahh! You mean the one that was disabled just this morning."

"I'm supposed to report to my Capo every day at this time, he'll notice something fishy if I don't and then-"

She cut him off by flashing the latest news from her burner phone:

"Is the well-reputed gentleman, Santano Giovanni, secretly involved in a drug cartel? Research revealed there was Methamphetamine, a highly addictive and illegal psychostimulant drug similar to amphetamine, laced in his company's newly released coffee that was said to increase wakefulness and allow higher levels of physical activity, aimed largely towards students and-" She turned it off.

Alfonzo's face was crumpled and he tried to push down the lump in his throat.

"What do you think? Will he come for you or something that's actually important? At the end of the day, aren't you quite disposable?"

She watched in delighted rapture as the light in his eyes dimmed when he realised how hopeless his situation was. Santano would be too busy doing damage control due to the information leak to spare a thought for Alfonzo.

She had to thank Selene for that one.

As a last resort, he tried running away, flinging the blanket with which he had been covering his body aside. The blanket fell on the floor in a pool and he ended up tripping over it, falling with a mighty thud.

Jeez.

She winced inside, even as she asked him with hope in her eyes, "Did you, maybe, break any bones?"

He scoffed, standing up with a puffed-up chest as if to show how very sturdy he was.

Completely forgetting that he was in his birthday suit.

Lily was going to get a headache. "Put some clothes on, I beg you, you're causing visual pollution here."

He was about to protest but she pulled out her gun and pointed it towards him. "I'm a pretty good shot, you know."

Once he was decently clothed, she whacked her gun against his head, knocking him out.

She brought him to the living room; his body dripping with blood and his face indistinguishable when she was done.

He crawled on the ground, trying to move away. His wet hands made a splattering sound every time they collided with the floor. Maybe he was trying to tell her something but his jaws were broken - courtesy of her Prada heels, of course. His hands trembled, acting as a fountain of blood ever since she tore his nails off, one by one, drenching the once white marble floor red.

Bringing a glass from the kitchen, she held out his hands over it - the blood plunged in, filling the glass in no time. She tilted the wine glass and the red liquid seemed to sparkle.

Smiling a splendid smile, she held it out to him. "Drink."

Alfonzo recoiled, as much as he could, when he heard her. His beady eyes widened in disgust.

Her smile turned cruel. "What? Can't handle your enemy's blood once it's no longer metaphorical?"

She forced it against his mouth. "I thought of going the dramatic way and drinking and bathing with your blood myself like I see done in movies but then I thought, why should I pollute myself? So you drink it."

When he still resisted, she brought her silver dagger to his groin and raised an eyebrow.

Terror entered his clouded eyes as he took the glass with shaking fingers and desperately gulped down the contents. Some liquid escaped, giving an unrecognisable look to his already mangled features.

The stench of blood in the room was so thick, she could have stabbed it with her dagger. Pools of blood decorated the marble floor and smeared over the furniture.

With an intense gaze on him, she waited till the glass was empty.

And then there was a sound of the air being cut through as a small dagger rushed past and firmly planted itself on Alfonzo's heart.

Lily inspected her hands while he lay there, bleeding to death. A calmness entered her heart.

Trickles of blood streamed down her arms and dripped down from her elbows.

Lily stared, transfixed.

Taking a deep breath, she then glanced over at her phone on the table in the corner. She turned on the phone in the wake of more than twenty missed calls and over a hundred messages from Selene.

A sickening feeling took over her being as she clicked to see the latest texts:

I swear, Lily, get out of that place.

NOW.

But it was too late.

The sound of the door being slammed open travelled to her ear. There were multiple footsteps, all in coordination as if a small army was arriving in here.

If her life was a horror movie, this would be the place the protagonist died.

As if everything played out in slow motion, she turned her head, inch by inch, towards the men - her heart thumping so violently, it might have left her ribcage.

She was standing at the very corner of the room, with her wild hair and bloody hands. The evidence of her murdering someone right in front of her, having bled to death.

Her eyes trailed up to the man in front and she almost lost her grip on the phone.

Because in front of her, with a gaze as chilling as an ocean on a winter night, stood a man with a lean figure exuding an abnormal amount of confidence along with pure killing intent, his dark hair framing his elegantly tilted face as bewitchingly as those long lashes framed his mahogany eyes.

Well... this is probably my favourite chapter ending!

What will Blaise's reaction be?

Chapter 16

U nease had spread through Blaise when Lilithe did not pick up his calls. It only increased in concentration with her last text to him.

The image of her wronged and haunted eyes, with a thinly veiled hatred in them, staring over at the head of the Giovanni Corporation - it had felt as if the screen would melt due to her pure, volcanic rage.

A suspicion inside of him had taken root that night.

That suspicion only blared a loud, red signal when he was inundated with the information leak, the airing of the dirty laundry behind the official Giovanni company's newest product.

Along with it, Santano Giovanni's face was dragged through the mud.

Blaise wondered if he should feel regretful or perhaps guilty as, after all, Santano was nothing but a puppet - the real owner of the company was himself.

Santano was taking the fall for him.

Blaise thought back to Ruby Wraith who had been targeting the men in the Giovanni family for a few years now. His mind flashed back to the overflowing poison in Lilithe's forest green eyes.

He recalled the incident of the warehouse burning as Enrique was killed. Then he wondered about the coincidental scandal that, once again, had Santano and his men occupied. Distracted.

Reclined on a chair in the Giovanni mansion, he calmly watched Santano furiously try to deal with the scandal over the phone with his men flanking him.

Calculating eyes looked around the room. A strange feeling of being watched pervaded his senses.

Once the call ended, Blaise asked him, "Are all of your men here?"

"Alfonzo's taken a vacation, Boss. Should I call him back?"

Blaise tilted his head sideways. "Did you talk to him today? Will the current situation put him in danger?"

Santano shook his head with confidence but Blaise thought it was sheer stupidity. "His vacation villa is well guarded. I'll be informed as soon as something happens."

Because that worked so well last time.

Blaise stood up from his seat, glancing at him with curled lips. "I trust you to deal with your own mess, then."

Santano's face paled. "Yes, boss."

With a group of his men, he was off to the villa where Alfonzo Giovanni was supposedly vacationing.

Because try as he might, Blaise could not weed out the suspicion taking root in his heart.

A smile stretched over his face as he saw the dead bodyguards and how morbidly quiet the place was. So the information leak was a distraction.

He entered through the front door and stopped in front of the closed door of the living room. One of his men, a tall guy with a muscular frame, kicked the door open with a resounding slam.

A metallic smell diffused towards him - one he was all too familiar with his whole life.

He glanced around at splattered pools of blood and then at the corpse with a dagger stuck to his chest.

Sure enough, Ruby Wraith was at play.

Yet, his heartbeat doubled as he trailed his eyes to the corner of the room.

She was a vision both disturbing and alluring. With wild raven locks and blood dripping down her hands. Her forest green eyes turned more poisonous the longer she stared at him.

At that moment, there was a pain in his heart. A deep, agonising pain.

He had never hated being right so much before.

Somewhere during their staring contest, one of his men had gotten impatient. He was taking steps towards Ruby Wraith, no, towards Lilithe, loading his gun. "Boss, this is the bitch who stirred up all this trouble. We finally got her."

Bitch?

Lilithe quickly glanced at the gun in the man's hand but before she had the time to react, two gunshots rang louder than a siren.

Blaise watched as the gun flew out from the man's hand and one of his legs crumpled as he fell down on one knee.

The fallen man looked back at him from his position with no colour on his face but fear written on it as Blaise calmly put away the gun he had fired and asked, "Since when did my men start thinking on their own? I certainly do not remember ordering any of you to harm her."

Blaise raised up his eyes from the ground and rested them back on the dark beauty in front of him. She was scrutinizing him with everything she had in her.

Her eyes were venomous, with thinly veiled uncertainty.

He took large strides towards her and her hands were tightly clenched shut. Her body stiffened as if in preparation for the worse.

That spot in his heart hurt again.

With a proper distance between them just so she did not feel uncomfortable and restrained, he stopped.

A tentative and gentle smile broke through without his permission as the storm in his eyes was subdued with softness. His voice was light as he asked, "Would you like to freshen yourself?"

A quark of the poison in her eyes dissolved, taken over by more uncertainty. She looked over at his men, then look back at him, with lightly furrowed eyebrows.

He signalled at his men to leave.

Once the room was empty, save for the corpse on the floor, Blaise handed her a teasing smile - his voice, a soothing murmur. "Is it normal for you to forget how to speak after a fresh murder? Do you need some time to get your alphabet in order?"

Her shoulders relaxed unbeknownst to her.

But the battle had only started.

The poison made way for a look of bleak realization to enter her dense forest eyes, threatening to set the greenery ablaze. "The Giovanni Family is working with you."

Blaise hesitated.

"More like working under me Lilithe," he tried to assure. "It's different."

If he thought calling her Lilithe might remove that bleak expression from her eyes, he was wrong.

"Did you know about this?" She asked in a quiet, yet steady tone. "Did you know about me from the beginning?"

"If you're referring to Ruby Wraith, then not at all. I had no idea you were the one who burned down my warehouse."

Lilithe tightly closed her eyes shut as her nails mercilessly dug into her own flesh. "The company..."

"It is my own," he admitted. "Santano is just the marionette who will take the fall in case something drastic takes place. All the finalization documents were in paper to fend against hacking."

A humourless chuckle escaped her. "The barrier between you and ruination, then. He's quite important."

"Not quite," he carefully said. "I have many men available for the job so he is pretty disposable."

She chuckled again, a mocking edge to it.

"I knew you had an ulterior motive for killing Lorenzo in that alley. It couldn't possibly be only because you saw a woman in trouble. So it turns out you were venting your anger." She glanced up at him, her eyes no longer a forest green but rather, a poison green and he barely refrained from flinching. "Pretending to be kind and sincere must have felt amazing. Pretending to have nothing to gain from me must have felt amazing."

The more she spoke, the more urgently he felt he had to stop her. He had to explain. She was gradually reaching the brink and she might never return. His coldblooded eyes had long melted and all that remained was a desperation to be believed and trusted.

"The thought of lying to you does not feel good, Lily, so I will tell you this: Yes, I had ulterior motives before but now I only care for you. My link to the Giovanni Family does not matter, nor does you being Ruby Wraith." He watched as she took a deep breath and steadily released it.

"I believe you," she said her face uncomfortably blank.

He knew she was lying.

He still smiled at her in relief.

If she was willing to pretend, he could still take the time to slowly turn that pretence into reality.

"But I've been here long enough. This room stinks." Saying so, she swiftly turned away and strode towards the open door. "Do me a favour and get the woman locked in one of those rooms out safely."

With wide eyes, he stared at her wild, bloody appearance and walked along with her. "Surely, you're not leaving like this?"

She further sped up her pace, leaving him behind, and said in a tone that sounded like an order, "Don't follow me."

Though every cell in his body protested against it, Blaise listened to her.

She needed time. He could only give it to her.

He would wait until she was ready to talk to him without that bleakness in her eyes or that humourless tag to her laugh because that pain he felt when his suspicion was confirmed was due to the crippling feeling of failure that rushed through him once he realized he had been feeding the dogs who left her restless and escaping.

He needed to slowly dismember all the links between the Roosevelts and the Giovannis.

Lilithe must never even get the chance to entertain the thought that he might choose to keep profiting off of Santano over her.

After all, what was the loss of a few billion over quenching that throat-burning thirst for her revenge?

There you have it!

What'd you think about Blaise's reaction? Did you expect it or not?

This chapter was one of the hardest ones for me to write. I need to calculate which information to let out and which one to keep for later. I needed to organise everything each of them needed to know about the other but also keep the conversation between them flowing naturally.

Chapter 17

L ily barged into the penthouse, the sleek obsidian door ricocheting off the wall. Maybe her bloody hands left an imprint on the door but the dark colour made it hard to distinguish.

Just like the bleeding wound deep inside her battered and bruised heart.

How come she was so shaken up?

Wasn't she already used to betrayal by now? Didn't she disillusion herself long ago with fairy tales where people were sincere and true?

So why the hell was she so shaken up?

She found Selene in the living room, for once, not curled up delicately on the sofa while reading a book. Rather, pacing on the floor like nothing short of wearing a hole to it would calm her down.

Her body stiffened as she detected her presence.

As Selene swiftly turned to face her, Lily thought her eyes looked frostier than usual but more brittle, as if the ice would crack by the slightest bit of force, intentional or otherwise.

"So she finally remembers to come back." If Lily didn't know Selene better she would think there was a biting edge to her tone. But Selene wouldn't be that upset over this.

If Lily died, wouldn't it only free her from debt?

"How did you know?" Lily asked, referring to the millions of text messages warning her against the upcoming intruders.

"How did you not see my texts?"

"Iclyn," she said, her voice taking on an almost desperate tone.

It must be rare to see her in such a pathetic state, for Selene - stubborn, unmoving Selene - gave way. "I had a bad feeling the moment you left. So I hacked into the cameras inside the Giovanni mansion... guess who I saw lazily reclining on the armchair as if he owned the place."

Selene looked away from her, slim fingers toying with her platinum locks and continued, "I don't know why I did not get anything when I hacked in before. How could I not find out his involvement with Santano..."

"It was all done it paper. There was nothing you could've done," Lily interrupted before Selene could go down a path of self-doubt. Selene had always been pretty proud of her particular skill so this was a huge blow.

Sharp, cold eyes locked in with hers immediately. "And you know that because...?"

Lily sighed. "You asked me about the texts. Well, I didn't realise my phone was in silent mode."

Selene's round blue eyes widened a negligible amount but to those who knew her, that slight widening was a milestone reached. "You met him there? You met Blaise Roosevelt with your hands dripping with the blood of his subordinate?"

With her huge icy eyes and puffed squishy cheeks, Selene at the moment looked like a cuddly doll anyone would want to squeeze. Her tiny clenched fists only added to that effect.

But Lily couldn't feel anything beyond the uncomfortable churning in the pit of her stomach.

Why was Selene getting so worked up? Why wasn't she calmly reading her novels, as usual, and scolding her with disdain in her cold blue eyes?

Why did she change?

Why did everyone in her life change these days?

But perhaps Selene was only worried because she herself might become collateral if Blaise decided to come for Ruby Wraith, now that he knew who she was.

Surely, the reason behind her getting so worked up was due to deep-seated instincts of self-preservation.

That made more sense.

Calming herself down with that logic, Lily said, "He didn't harm or scare me. Nor did he threaten me. He said he didn't care who I was. He said Santano didn't matter. But the Giovanni family is his main source of money. He wanted me to believe him. But I burned down his warehouse and almost ruined his company so I don't believe him. I can't afford to."

Selene patiently listened to her rant, staring at her with those cold eyes and in Lily's mind, they steadily changed colour and turned a soothing shade of mahogany.

She was gradually taken back to only an hour ago in a room diffused with the metallic stench of blood.

There had been horror mingling with a deep-rooted fear sailing in his chilling mahogany eyes.

Why was there horror and fear if he wasn't planning something deplorable against her? Maybe he was afraid she would now see through him and ruin his plans!

She used to feel soothed by the bloodcurdling promise displayed in those irises.

But not then.

Not when she had stood before him as exposed as she had been that night, running for her life with nothing but her two scarred legs.

Not when all she had felt at that moment was a crippling unease every time she glanced into those eyes long molten into something tentatively tender.

If she admitted she had been afraid at that moment, would she be mocked for it?

Because tenderness and care had been the exact emotions swimming in the eyes of the people who had taken her in, after her parents' death.

As it turned out, her body needed to pay for basking in their care.

"Nothing in the world is free, sweet Rose," a revolting voice had crooned. "How do you plan on paying us back for caring for you all this time?"

After seven years in their hands, there was only so much of her left to pay with. How could she afford to settle the debts of a Mafiaso?

How much more would she have to sacrifice?

In the end, what if crumbs were the only thing that was left of her otherwise phantom spirit? Who would spend their time picking up the scattered shards in the aftermath of the eruption?

Then next time, what if those shards were no longer sharp?

What if they were blunt and useless, like the echo that remained?

She might have glued herself together once, but she couldn't do it again.

So even though the tenderness in his eyes was enough to unfurl butterflies in her stomach, it was also enough to freeze her blood.

Even though she had wanted to lose herself in those gentle waves, she also wanted to sail away from them. Before the sky darkened and the lightning flashed. Before the once gentle waves turned harsh and unyielding, leaving her with no escape but to drown.

She didn't want to drown again.

She had been trapped in his eyes in that room and she had wanted to run away.

Blood was dripping from her hands but this time they weren't Alfonzo's. She had been digging her nails in her palms so ferociously, she was surprised to not have noticed sooner.

The scenery gradually evolved into her home. Selene was still in her position, having witnessed her whole turmoil with her unflinching eyes.

"You really have no more faith in humanity, do you?" Selene asked in a somber tone.

Lily flashed her a tired smile. "No more than you do."

"But these days... These days I thought..." Selene trailed off but Lily's eyes sharpened.

"You thought what?"

Selene's emotionless eyes studied her for some time and maybe it was the exhaustion etched into her face or maybe it was the fragile look coating the usual wildness in her eyes but Selene let out a soft sigh. "Nevermind, Lily. You should wash up. You have had a tiring day."

As Selene left, Lily took tentative steps towards the glass windows, gazing out at the shadows beyond.

The night sky was a blanket of obsidian, covering everything with darkness. The stars were dimming with every second that passed, forming lonely and empty spaces, reflecting sadness and despair. The moon cast a muted light, revealing and magnifying. In Lily's eyes, the night sky seemed to acknowledge its loss, grief and regret.

If only...

Over the next few days, she tried to convince Selene to go into hiding. And failed to do so.

The only thing she did was incorporate a stronger security system.

But Lily failed to see how that was better than going into hiding. What if Blaise just bombed the building? Or something that might work its way around the system?

Could one even bomb a building that had a highly efficient security system or would the bomb be discovered before exploding? Lily had no idea, her knowledge did not extend to these things.

But Selene's knowledge did and she did not think the situation warranted such a drastic method.

And as days passed without any attempt at assassination like Lily had feared or any public statement exposing Ruby Wraith, Selene grew more adamant about living like normal.

She kept saying that she had a feeling nothing bad was going to happen this time.

Even though Lily was less than satisfied with the arrangement she had long learned to not doubt the power of Selene's intuition.

Still, she made sure to pinch Selene's chubby cheeks at least once every day as a form of revenge.

Watching her face scrunch up cutely was a priceless sight to behold.

But by the second week's end, Lily grew tired of acting like a coward and hiding. Because how long will she keep it up? How long could she keep it up?

Problems wouldn't disappear just because she hid from them.

She needed to get out and murder her problems. Very thoroughly so that they wouldn't be able to get up ever again.

In her contact list where the name 'Blaise' flashed out to her, still laid the last text she'd sent him, asking him to not bother her.

At that time, she hadn't expected him to barge into the room she was in, instead.

He wanted her to believe him.

So why didn't he reach out even once?

Was he playing a game now, where she was his amusing pawn?

Whatever it was, she needed answers. And Lily wasn't the type of person who would stay cooped up and waiting.

Before, she was too shaken up to think straight.

But now she wanted answers.

So on the first day of the third week, she decided to confront him.

When she told Selene, all that the ice blonde said was: "Don't die. I have not yet repaid my debt to you."

That was an easy enough requirement to fulfil.

"I'm not so easy to kill as that, Selene. Crawled out of death's door once and sure as hell can do it again. Besides." She gave a vengeful smirk. "I have yet to make Santano regret the day he was born."

The next chapter will be about Lily meeting Blaise! What are you expecting? :)

Chapter 18

Lily stepped out of her Ferrari and found herself in front of a large iron gate. As she stepped through, her eyes danced across the shrubs and flowers decorating the land. In the middle was a fountain proudly flowing with crystals of water, shining as the golden rays glided over them.

She followed the gravel path that led to the main entrance, admiring the statues and sculptures that dotted the garden like silent guardians keeping watch. The mansion looming over all, ancient but elegant, took her back to a time described only in the classics.

She supposed it made sense for a man burrowing himself in those books to have a home that was a reflection of it.

She walked up the stairs to the door but she did not need to knock or ring for the door was opened from the inside on its own.

So she strode in, not once faltering in her confident strides.

The hanging chandeliers sparkled, casting shadows at angles.

Once inside, she looked up the flight of marble stairs and there, looking as if he was on top of the world, with a confidence in his gait that matched her own, stood Blaise Roosevelt.

He tilted his head, glancing at her who stood below him, and because she refused to be below anyone, she speedily walked up the stairs, levelling him with her daring gaze.

"So she finally comes out of hiding," he said, raising an elegant brow. "I suppose my days of waiting with agony were worth it."

She scoffed in reply. "I was never in hiding."

Which was an utter lie, of course, but Lily remained shameless.

He let her keep her pride intact, playing along like, as she'd come to realise, he always did. No matter what ridiculous or diabolical thing she did or said.

He led her to his office and they both took a seat.

He was observing her for long enough that she was ready to say, 'I get that I'm gorgeous but you need to pay if you stare that long.'

But then he remarked in a light tone, "You did not bring any weapons and you don't look nervous. That must mean you trust me at least a little."

"I don't."

But she wanted to.

So she took a little risk. After all, frolicking with danger had always been her dearest hobby.

She spoke up again before he could. "I came here to get answers. I wasn't in the right... mental state that day so I could only go along with you."

"You told me you believed me."

"I'm sure you realized it was a lie. I do not believe you," she said slowly. "Not even a little bit."

There was a storm taking place in his ruthless gaze that was half-hidden by his fluttering long lashes.

"I know." The voice was soft and understanding. "I would not believe me either, given my reputation, let alone you who weathered the worst cyclones."

"You're very different today," she accused. "You were very different that day as well."

His eyes had been molten with tenderness and care.

She hated it.

"Was I?" he raised an eyebrow in amusement. "I am always like this."

She narrowed her eyes and then stood up as if to leave. His hand flung out and grasped her arm in a firm grip, yet, as she stared down at the place where his skin met hers, he quickly let go.

"Alright, alright. I'll admit, I was playing along with you before so you wouldn't be as jittery as you are now. I could not afford to let you leave me be, now could I?"

Her eyes blazed with outrage. "Are you trying to tell me that all those moments-"

"No. Sorry for interrupting you but no, Lilithe. I know what you are thinking and I think you should stop. Because none of it was fake or forced. I enjoyed every moment of our time together. Don't you dare even contemplate otherwise because where you hiding from me for weeks did not manage to do so, this contemplation will break me." There was an intently unyielding strength beneath his words, one that refused to bend under the utmost pressure.

She didn't know this tone.

He hadn't spoken to her that way before, never with that much authority.

She knew the words he'd said just now were meant to be taken gravely by her. He wasn't playing around.

And because she was in his house and surrounded by his people, she decided to be smart and not argue for once in her life.

"Fine, let's pretend it really was quite real in your eyes. Why go through the trouble in the first place? I'm assuming it's not because you saw me and wanted to possess me by any means possible."

"You assume so many heinous things about me but not this?" His rosy lips curled up in a mild smile.

She looked at him, annoyed. "You blush whenever I get near you looking like the guy version of Rapunzel locked in a tower who never saw a person of the opposite gender before."

His eyes widened and he had the gall to protest against her treatment of him. "That, Lilithe, is a violation of human rights."

"You keep calling me Lilithe. I don't remember giving you permission."

"Alright then, Lily. I will listen to you."

"Then answer my damn question."

She watched as heaviness made way in his molten mahogany eyes, slowly hardening them back to ruthlessness.

She wondered why she felt a pang in her heart and a glimmer of nostalgia sweeping through.

"It was your eyes," he said, keeping his gaze on his hands. "Your tortured eyes, thinly veiled with insanity and craze. Did you think nobody would notice?"

He looked back up, staring straight at her, sending goosebumps traveling through her skin. "Because I noticed, Lily. They held the same expression as my mother's eyes right after my... father left our house each day."

There was a current, electrifying in an unpleasant way, that was buzzing through her veins.

She remembered Selene offhandedly commenting before. About how the previous boss' murder might have to do with the wife.

She understood it now.

Selene's hunch was always right. She had this sixth sense that Lily really envied.

As someone who experienced the same horrifying experience, a piece of her well-guarded heart squeezed out and went out to that woman.

But the more prominent emotion Lily experienced at that moment was nausea, slow and creeping, once she realized that he knew, Blaise knew what happened to her.

Her nails dug into the silk cloth of the sofa she was sitting on. But her face remained carefully blank. She was not going to lose control this time. She was not going to leave again.

Blaise's eyes remained on her through it all. His expression was apologetic, yet understanding. "That was my main ulterior motive. The warehouse being a minor one. I have come clean, Lily. I swear this was all."

"You could be saying this to gain sympathy."

His eyes were sorrowful. "I am really not."

But Lily couldn't believe him completely. No matter how much she wanted to, she just couldn't. She might as well have been a robot with being untrusting of his sincerity programmed into her.

"That is to say, because of this you don't even care who I am and the sheer amount of money I've caused you to lose? Am I the only one who thinks it sounds utterly unrealistic? Am I going crazy here?"

"It's not unrealistic if I care for you, Lily," Blaise said in a whisper. "I want to help you. You turning out to be Ruby Wraith just makes it easier. If you were a normal citizen, my methods might have been too gruesome for you but now I do not have to worry about these meagre things."

But in her mind, the only words that rang louder than a tinkling bell were 'care' and 'help'.

He cared? He wanted to help?

She let out a cynical laugh. "You care for me, Blaise?"

"I do," he said with steel in his tone.

"You want to help me?"

"You don't believe it?"

"What do you want in return?" she asked, her features arranged to a sneer.

Blaise blinked, those long lashes fluttering innocently.

"You will help me for what cost? What do I have to give up? What do I have to sacrifice? How many pieces of my soul do I have to scatter about before the world is satisfied?"

"Lily..."

"Don't say that you want nothing. I won't believe it, I won't. That's what everyone says at the start. That's what they said." She breathed in faster, refusing to acknowledge the trembling of her hands and they dug in further into the silk sofa.

She only glared at him with as much hate as she could summon from her tired and depleted body.

Why was she so tired?

She'd felt rejuvenated earlier this morning.

A flash of realization entered his coldblooded eyes before, in front of her own eyes, he transformed into the man she was familiar with before all hell had broken loose on her tail.

He let out a friendly smile and asked indifferently, "Nothing? Who said I wanted nothing?" He tilted his head to the side, eyes glinting dangerously. "In fact, I want something only you can give. No one else will do."

Her heart slowed watching the dangerous spark in his eyes and the open expression back on his face. It wasn't logical, her body's reaction. In her head, she was aware that he was probably intentionally doing this, and that he could just as easily go back to his unsettlingly tender look. But when it came to this, she was helpless as her anxiety bubbled down.

"So what's it you want?"

He leaned towards her. His voice was low and electrifying. His tone, threatening.

"Your happiness."

He held up a hand before she could burst out in another bout. "Think of it from my perspective, Lily. Your happiness is my happiness. You came into my life and made it all revolve around you. And now, there is no me without you." A strand of his hair fell over his eyes and she watched as he pushed it back. "So in order to ensure my happiness, I am considering yours. That is my gain from all of it. When you actually think about it, I am being quite selfish and insincere. You probably shouldn't trust me at all as all I am after is my happiness."

By the time he was finished, he stared at her with those callous eyes, completely serious about the nonsense he'd just spoken.

Someone who had his own selfish agenda was more trustworthy in Lily's eyes than one who claimed to want nothing in return.

Thinking about it carefully, Lily supposed he did have a point. She actually could trust him as he will ensure her happiness for his own.

But looking at his half-molten, half-solid eyes, she couldn't shake the growing feeling that maybe he was playing her for a fool.

But if he was, Lily would sweep it under the rug as she did with everything that bothered her.

After all, she really did want to trust him.

And now she just found an excuse to.

They finally had an honest, much-needed, conversation! Lily doesn't trust him yet but wants to. Blaise... I hope he'll have fun waiting for her :)

Chapter 19

Revenge was a dish best served cold.

Who knew it better than Lily?

She had bid her time, patiently waiting and planning, then slowly ripping them, thread by thread. She had made sure, when the time arrived, her needle was sharp and pointy.

Considering all that, wasn't it the height of stupidity that she contemplated trusting Blaise after he laid low for weeks, instead of taking revenge on her for all that she's done to him?

It was, after all, only a few weeks.

Lily had waited for years to exact her revenge.

What if he was just waiting for the right time?

But she wanted to trust him.

(And she didn't know why.)

Maybe her propensity for danger finally broke her. Lily had always been a little careless. But she was never this reckless.

"You were right," she said, rushing into the living room where Selene sat, reading a novel.

"I am right about most things, Lilithe. Which, in particular, are you talking about?" She put away her book and levelled her with that cool gaze.

"His mother. He killed his dad for her." She was going to say more but then hesitated, staring at the abandoned novel on the sofa.

"Lily?" Her gaze snapped towards Selene. "What's wrong?"

Lily hoped the way her fingers dug into the velvet cloth wasn't too noticeable. She hoped Selene didn't realize her hands were trembling.

"He knows," she said, her voice low and at an edge. "He knew what happened to me ever since he met me."

Selene remained silent, likely processing the entire thing.

"He told me it was because of his mother," Lily added with pursed lips, gradually calming herself down while glancing at the calm Selene.

"You sound like you do not believe it."

Lily sighed. "Among all the things he's said, I'm closest to believing this one. His entire demeanour changed in a way I could relate to."

But if he lied to her about this, they could never go back.

It would be too great a gashing wound.

He had told her so many things back in his office. He told her he wanted her happiness. He also told her he was always just playing along.

That explained why there was no attraction involved in the beginning.

That only evolved once he got to know her.

"He said he wanted my happiness," Lily spoke up, once again. "Because it will aid in his happiness."

Selene stared at her for the next few minutes, only blinking every so often, before gathering up the book she'd thrown aside. "This Blaise is quite a character. I want to see him."

"You've already seen him."

"I want to talk to him."

"Why the sudden desire?"

"Just do as I say and bring him over."

"You can't be serious." Lily's eyes widened. "I thought I was the crazy one. You want me to bring him, the mafia boss who I'm not even fully sure if I can trust, here in our home? In our safe haven?"

"Cut the drama, Lilithe. You did it before, what is so different this time?" Selene raised an imperceptive eyebrow. "Don't worry. I have a feeling everything will work out fine."

For someone so cold and emotionless, she sure had a lot of those feelings.

Lily was going to object more but her phone rang, demanding her attention instead.

When she saw the words 'Straitlaced Max' flashing, she ignored it like she always did.

"That stuffy jerk, again?"

"Yep," Lily said, putting away the phone. "It was fun before but he's become a headache these days. Remind me again why I thought it was a good idea to get involved with him?"

"He was on your case and you being you, thought it would be cool to date someone who wants you jailed?"

Lily shrugged in reply. Guilty as charged.

She must have a death wish.

That was the sentence whirling around Lily's head as she stepped into his territory, once again.

But what was a girl to do when her one and only support pushed her into the pit? She hoped Blaise didn't mind people barging in unannounced.

Because that was exactly what she was doing right now.

As she stood before the looming mansion, her mind took her back to the last time she arrived. Although there had been confidence in her gait, her insides were jittery, with uncertainty swimming throughout.

Her brain had been thrown into a confused mess from then on.

And when she rose to leave, he had done the same, just as quickly. Rapidly. As if afraid, if he was a little slow, she'd be gone before he could do much.

His hands were clenched, tightly holding onto the back of his chair. "You are confused right now. Come back when you sort things out by yourself?"

But in his eyes, the reluctance had been displayed as clear as the ocean.

The door opened, bringing her back to the present, revealing a woman with hair of spun gold and fair skin. She was about to step out when her eyes caught Lily's.

Lily glanced behind the woman where Blaise stood, his eyes holding surprise, and if she dug deeper, joy. "Lily..."

Her legs moved on their own toward them.

"This is Lily? That Lily? The Lily you're obsessed with?" The woman looked at Blaise with a smile that seemed to be a little too sly.

"Yes, mom." Although he seemed embarrassed to be put on the spot about something like this. When he continued, looking directly at herself, he was calm and resolute. "She's the Lily I am obsessed with."

Lily would have teased him if he got flustered, unable to reply, but faced with his direct gaze, whatever reply she came up with got stuck in her throat. She could only give him a smirk before focusing on the woman before him. His mother.

Knowing the tall, beautiful woman before her, the one who seemed so warm and cheerful, went through, to some extent, the same thing as herself, Lily unknowingly softened her tone. "So you're his mother. He spoke about you quite often."

Lips stretched in a smile, her golden hair shined in the sunlight. "Call me Violette. And what are we doing standing out here? Come inside." Saying so, she gave Blaise a look that had him rushing to Lily's side, guiding her inside.

... Lily has to say, she really liked Violette.

Lily meets Violette! Also, what do you think Selene's up to?

Is Blaise going to start getting bolder now? :)

Chapter 20

Time passed quickly with the three of them.

Violette had a liveliness about her that complimented her own, quite well. Blaise jokingly brought up how he felt like the third wheel here when they were fully immersed in their conversation.

Even though the slight unease Lily had felt when she entered the house subsided in the wake of Violette's shining smiles, she never forgot her own plans.

When she tactfully brought up the matter with the previous Boss of the Italian mafia, Violette's smiles that shined so bright till now dimmed considerably.

Nightmares clouded her eyes.

Lily couldn't remember the last time she felt guilty for any questionable thing she did, might have even forgotten the feeling of having that particular emotion pass through.

But at that moment, she felt guilty. For bringing up such a sensitive topic, even if it was for an understandable reason. For making Violette's nightmares come up again, even if it wasn't her intention.

And when Blaise interfered, cautiously changing the topic to a much better direction, Lily wanted to hug that man in gratitude.

Guilt was such an uncomfortable feeling. If she never felt guilty again, it'd be too soon.

Violette left soon after remarking, "I'll leave you two lovebirds to romance each other, then."

Lily strongly wanted to protest against it. She was no lovebird! How cheesy did that sound?

But the woman left before she could garner her properly indignant response.

She could only look at Blaise, with grievances written in her eyes.

Light laughter spilt from his lips. "I've never seen you on the losing side of a talk before. I can only apologize on behalf of my mother."

She rolled her eyes. "Whatever. And you don't need to apologise for your mother. I quite like her." She then shrugged. "I'm not a sore loser."

But now that it was back to the two of them again, memories of their previous few encounters surfaced. Lily wasn't someone familiar with the word: Awkward. Wherever she went, awkwardness fled in the opposite direction.

Today seemed to be a day where she was experiencing a lot of novelties.

She only came back to this place because... because Selene told her to!

But if she told him that, he would think she didn't want to come here which... would it hurt his feelings? He did say he... cared for her. Which is probably a lie! She shouldn't take it seriously. And... and... why did she need to be honest about her purpose in coming here? She could just lie and he wouldn't be hurt and wait-

Why would she care if he was hurt or not? What did it matter to her?

Oh, that's right! He could decide to retaliate against her if he felt wronged in any way.

Right! Exactly!

Relief coursed through her veins even as she foresaw a massive headache later on from overthinking so much. Being around Blaise might be bad for her health. She should limit herself from now on.

She didn't want to die so young and beautiful.

"Lily...?"

She snapped her head back up to look at him.

A spellbound smile was playing on his lips. "What's wrong? You are very absentminded."

Your fault.

Blaise raised an eyebrow, the picture of innocence. "Me? What have I done?"

... The audacity some people have.

A sigh escaped his lips as if he had suffered many grievances but was choosing to make peace with them. "Nevermind. I will let your hurtful implications pass since you have been on good behaviour so far."

And then he stopped, realising something. He narrowed his eyes at her but she could see the playfulness in his eyes. "That's right. You have been on suspiciously good behaviour so far."

"While your behaviour is degrading very fast. What?" Lily stood up. "Did you want me to start screaming and throwing things around?"

She walked around and picked up a crystal vase. "If I do start throwing things, it's going to be done at you."

Blaise leisurely glanced from the vase on her hands to her face. "That's alright, Lily." A mild smile played on his lips. "I like you just as you are, not screaming and throwing things around."

"Ahhh..." Lily showed a contemplative face before purposefully raising the vase. "That's more of a reason for me to do this, then."

"Well, I'm going to like you regardless of your evolution." He shrugged. "You are stuck with me no matter what you do."

Looking at him leaning on the sofa in such a relaxed manner, Lily contemplated actually throwing the vase at him. She spent weeks with this man. But never before had she found him this annoying.

Was it a sign from the universe that her attraction towards him was fading away so she should cut her losses and move on?

"Yeah," she spoke up. "I'm sure you'll just follow me if I leave."

He suddenly no longer looked as composed, patches of pink dusting his fair cheeks and damnit, she lost her breath again. Yeah, okay, he might be more annoying now but that didn't seem to affect his attractiveness.

"That was for a good reason!"

"Sure, sure. Let's pretend so for now."

"For now? It truly was-"

"Moving on, Selene wants to see you." She paused. That might sound a bit ominous. "I mean, she'd like to invite you for... dinner."

He elegantly tilted his head. "You came all the way here just to tell me that? You could have texted."

She was going to do that. But then she didn't. For some reason.

"Why, you don't want me here? I can always leave if I'm not welcome-"

For the first time since she knew him, she caught a glimpse of panic in his callous eyes.

"That's NOT what I..." A sigh escaped him, seeing her suppressing a mischievous smile. "How do you manage to turn everything I say into an attack?"

She let out a laugh. "It's a talent."

"You are a talented woman."

"Do I smell sarcasm?"

"What is it with you and assuming the worst of me today? Or wait, any day?"

She looked out the window. "The sky's so blue today."

She heard a resigned chuckle from behind as she kept looking outside, unaware of the fond smile that was blooming on her lips.

Blaise chose violence today and so did Lily!

Chapter 21

"Why did you clean up after him?"

Blaise looked up at her in surprise. And blinked in confusion.

Lilithe was currently giving him a serious stare. Her mood did a whole one-eighty today.

"Who exactly...?"

"When the company was under fire, him being the main target, why did you wrap it up instead of leaving him to take the fall? You told me he wasn't important to you. That he was disposable. Or should I not believe a word you say?"

"That... was a quick change of mood, Lily. You ask me this now when we are both at your house, rather than yesterday when you were at mine. Is it that you feel safer here?" A light smile spread across his pink lips. "You think you can safely speak your mind here without anyone pointing a gun at you?"

Looking out into the sky, at the twinkling stars, he let out a heavy sigh; the callousness in his eyes was particularly sharp. "So this is what has been going through your mind?"

"I'm not wrong to ask." He heard her defensive voice speak up.

"Of course not, Lily." His tone was mild as he glanced back at her with a friendly expression. "I never said you were wrong. I was only blaming my own incompetence."

Some of that hardness in her eyes faded. Along with that, the tightness in his chest also slightly dissipated. Just like that, the air seemed fresher and he could breathe more easily.

"I was waiting for your input," he told her.

For a few seconds, a fire blazed out in those forest-green eyes. One that incinerated the remaining portions of hardness in them, leaving behind the ashes to form a web full of complicated feelings.

"My input?"

"You are the victim."

She looked at him like he was mentally challenged. "You make it sound so simple."

He tilted his head sideways. "It is not a simple thing?"

"He is one of you, Blaise. And I am-"

"Hold on. Sorry to interrupt but please don't lump him together with me. I do not care how involved he was with me before but now that I know what he did, given what happened to my own mother, how can you expect me to keep him with me?"

Lilithe looked away, pressing her lips together, sceptical and contemplating all at once. "So you're telling me... you're still keeping him alive and unscathed because you want me to decide what to do with him? You want me to deal with him?"

He raised a brow at her disbelieving tone. "Wasn't that your plan in the first place? Isn't that what Ruby Wraith always does?"

He then shrugged, nonchalantly. "Of course, during your stage of planning, if you want me to do anything to him, I will do so. I will help you in any way I can."

Lilithe let out a small laugh at that. One that sounded a little helpless. Like she was clueless on what to do about him. The guy in front of her who was spouting nonsense.

Blaise chose to not address that. Only time and sincerity will earn her trust. He could tell her about this all he wanted. She wouldn't believe him.

He was already considered to have lucked out so far since she was, at least, speaking to him (almost) like normal. Since she invited him to her house. This might not be the best-case scenario but it, thankfully, wasn't the worst-case scenario, either.

Blaise looked down at the velvet sofa they both sat on. The distance between them was much greater than it had been when he came here last time. Only a few months ago.

But it felt like forever.

It had been so long since Lilithe was relaxed around him. Even when she seemed to be, her shoulders would be just a little too stiff, her mischievous smile, a little too strained.

Even now, as he studied her side profile, she was in a comfortable pose, yet her eyes were alert, constantly looking around, not resting in one place for too long.

How much of her was true the previous day, and how much of it was her acting? He liked to think he was pretty good at reading her but now he wasn't so sure. He missed her being uneasy over his decision, or lack of thereof, on Santano. What else did he miss?

His musings were interrupted as Lily exclaimed, "Selene!" when the ice blonde entered the room.

He calmly looked up with an ever-present smile on his face, his own eyes locking with those frigid, blank ones.

Although both had the last name 'Blackthorne' and went by as sisters, Lilithe and the woman before him, Iclyn, could not be more different. While Lilithe was tall and voluptuous, with a sly smile etched on her face, Iclyne was of a slender build with a round, expressionless face.

And those eyes... he didn't have proper words to describe those unsettling eyes that held no emotions. It was almost inhumane. Like the person in front of him was but a machine. A humanoid robot.

It was deeply disconcerting. Not a feeling he got very often. But he would need to get used to it if he wanted to keep Lilithe in his life.

But given how shrivelled up he was inside even though he already met her twice before, that might not happen anytime soon. Especially if she kept giving him that dead stare.

"Lilithe," Iclyn spoke in a toneless voice. "Go help Mrs Crumb set the table."

"Why me?" Lilithe protested. "Couldn't you have done it before coming here?"

A few seconds passed.

Iclyn did not glance at Lilithe. She did not say anything either. But the silence was very telling. Lilithe looked at him and then looked at her. Coming to a conclusion, she nodded to herself. "Alright, fine. I'll set the table. Just for today. Since we have a guest. But I'll remember you never set the table for me even once."

Why was she glaring at him? What did he do?

"We never had dinner or lunch at my house."

She raised an unimpressed eyebrow.

"I can help you right now, if you want," he tried again.

She was about to open her mouth to respond when Iclyn spoke up, "If you want to be of help that much, you should keep me company while Lilithe is away."

Lilithe sighed in annoyance as Blaise gave her a helpless shrug.

"Did Lilithe mention that I wanted to see you?" asked Iclyn, eyes resting on him.

So long as one did not look too closely, all they would see when they looked at this woman was the innocent, angelic front. The light pink tops she wore, along with the silvery strands of hair that decorated her face only added to the image.

But Blaise wasn't one to be easily deceived.

Even though her face remained expressionless, he could almost see the wheels of her mind turning and calculating.

His lips curled lightly as he turned his head away from her, letting her gaze rest at his side profile, instead. "She did. She told me of your invite to dinner."

"I am not here to sound you out. You don't need to be so careful."

His relentless eyes once again met her unfeeling ones. His smile turned genial as he said, "What are you talking about? I don't think I understand."

He had been in situations like this before and this was the moment, when whoever he was with would start doubting their memory, doubting and rethinking, maybe they got it wrong, or maybe they were being too paranoid.

But the ice blonde before him indeed remained as composed as ice. "You and Lilithe are a good match. You both have that uncanny ability of bull-shitting your way out."

A laugh escaped his lips.

A good match, huh? Maybe when he stops messing up while trying to help her.

Those sharp eyes seemed to catch his inner turmoil. "It's not you."

"What's not me?"

"The thing that's happening between you two right now. The conflict. You are not the problem."

He looked away, pursing his lips, letting in a deep breath and then slowly letting it out.

"I'm not the problem? I'm always the problem," he murmured to himself, the storm in his mahogany eyes grew fiercer.

"You have some unresolved trauma? In any case, this particular problem isn't you. Lilithe just... doesn't believe in sincerity. She doesn't believe anyone in this world can be true to someone without having an ulterior motive. It's her personal thinking process so... do not blame yourself. No matter how carefully you treat her, you will keep being the object of her suspicion. So if you are the prideful or sensitive kind, you probably won't last long." Her head tilted sideways, eyes scrutinising him. "But I am telling you this because I am fully sure you aren't. I would hate to see you discouraged... and giving up."

What she said took a while for him to process. But once it did, his lips effortlessly stretched further. While his expression was just as amicable, the blizzard in his eyes had settled down.

He didn't want to assume too much and overstep but... was that her informing him of her support? She did not look like someone who would be that cooperative.

There was one thing he was quite curious about, however... "You are pretty sincere to her and she seems to-"

"I am here because I owe her. She knows that well. It's nothing more than that."

A soft laugh left him.

"She isn't the only one with a unique thinking process, now, is she?" his tone was amused. This was just fantastic. Is that why they stuck together? Both were good at pushing people away so found solace in each other?

Iclyn remained unruffled on the surface. But the icyness in her eyes grew tenfold. "I don't know what you mean."

"Who's bullshitting out of situations now?"

She gave him a withering look. "Why are you copying me? Do have some creativity."

"Look at people shamelessly changing the subject." Blaise sighed with heaviness.

"At the very least, I am not an uncreative copycat."

On the contrary to their ongoing conversation, the atmosphere surrounding them was lighter. The air was flowing with less tension and his guard wasn't quite as strict.

As he went back to his mansion after the dinner, thoughts rotated throughout his mind.

Looked like he had a backup now.

Well, well... Whatever is going to happen to Santano now... Blaise is no longer his backer (or so he says, Lily clearly has some trouble believing it).

But more importantly, despite meeting a few times before, this is the first actual conversation between Blaise and Iclyn. Looks like Iclyn is now officially a {Blaise X Lilithe} shipper.

Chapter 22

S o many thoughts whirled around in Lily's head as Blaise left. Many questions arose. Many times, she opened her mouth but before a word could get out, she closed it. When it came to Selene, there was no point asking.

If she wanted to tell, she would have done so unprompted.

Instead, the next time Lily opened her mouth, her tone had a lighthearted, teasing touch. "So how's it going with the men in your life?"

She was aware of Selene's sharp eyes on her, but she kept her back to the ice blonde, busying herself with doing the dishes.

"I have decided to take a break from dating."

A sudden huff of amusement left Lily as she whirled around to face her. "Dating? I'm sorry, when did you ever date? You're more of the..." Her voice trailed off and a coughing fit took over her at the absolutely withering look that tiny creature sent her.

Damn.

This is why you never judge a person by her appearance... or her height.

"My point is," Selene started indignantly. "They keep running away."

A wicked smile lurked on Lily's face. "I thought you were going to kidnap them?"

"With my size? I'd be better off kidnapping butterflies." Selene glanced away with a disdainful look in her cold blue eyes. "At least, they're pretty."

Blaise was positive he had been staring at the same page of his book for the last half an hour. A new day should come with new possibilities, new hopes and dreams, new worries and not the ones that followed him all the way from Lilithe's penthouse last night.

He was being ungrateful. He should be relieved she had decided to ask him, to confront him with her doubts about his intentions instead of disappearing from his life for weeks on end as she'd done before.

It was nothing.

He was just blowing things out of proportion, needlessly hurt when she didn't mean it. He was overreacting. He was being too sensitive.

It was just...

It was dumb. Her doubts were completely understandable. It was him. He was the one at fault.

You are not the problem.

Iclyn's cool voice rang through his head. It kept reverberating through every nook and cranny of his mind.

Frustrated, Blaise pinched the bridge of his nose. Fingers reached out to rest on his mildly throbbing temple.

A heavy sigh escaped him.

Lilithe just... doesn't believe in sincerity. Her words keep echoing. So... do not blame yourself.

Easier said than done.

It had only been a couple days, he told himself. Things will get better soon. He couldn't be so weak as to bow down so early on in the game.

She needed his resilience in the face of her doubts. She needed him to keep caring until she was ready to believe it.

Mostly, she needed him to... temper himself and not come on too strong.

But therein lay the problem.

That was the difficult part. Keeping a balance. A right balance.

The fall could be deadly if he wasn't careful. In this game of keeping-a-balance, he could lose much more than merely his life.

A ping cut through the tense silence. He looked over at his lit-up phone screen. A text from Lilithe popped up:

You up for lunch?

A light smile spread across his lips.

Let the game of balancing start.

They were both seated at a restaurant of Lilithe's choosing. The table was near the large glass walls, letting one look into the outside world.

There was a palpable sense of cheer and energy in the air. Customers were pouring in and out, constantly.

Lilithe was busy soaking in everything around her while Blaise carefully studied her.

Sunlight fell on her beautiful, dark curls, causing them to glisten with a warm, velvety shine. The light danced gently across their soft surface, creating tiny little sparkling highlights. Her eyes shone as if blazed by a forest fire. They held a certain slyness, a brewing mischief. One that put him at ease.

Those mischievous eyes were now looking straight at him, as her red lips painted a teasing smile. He blinked at the suddenness and looked down at his plate full of food.

Curse his light skin which made blushes easily noticeable.

"Why are you looking back down? You seemed to enjoy staring at me quite a lot."

He cleared his throat, getting his flustered state back in control before glancing back at her; a mild smile on his lips. "You provide an enjoyable scenery to stare at."

An involuntary huff of amusement escaped her. Her lips parted as she was about to reply but then her eyes caught on something behind him and her original reply was set aside by another.

"What a beauty." Her eyes wide in admiration.

He raised an intrigued eyebrow, using the glass in front of him as a mirror, he tilted it slightly to get a good view of the person who had Lilithe stupified.

The woman who entered had fiery red locks, draped over her shoulders. Tall and well-built, her features struck a perfect balance between angular and delicate. She had a pair of honey-coloured almond eyes that seemed all the more attractive due to the air of mystery shrouding her.

The woman was objectively beautiful. But objectively speaking, many people were beautiful.

"You almost pale in comparison." Still wide-eyed.

He cocked his head. "She's better looking than me?"

"Of course, not!" She hurriedly assured him. "You're still the most attractive one. The only person whose beauty you can't outshine is me." She let that thought sit for a while before continuing with a guileless smile. "But then again, my beauty is something mere mortals can't compete with so don't feel too bad."

"Thank you for the reassuring words, Lily. I feel much better now." An amused smile rested on his lips.

The following silence between them was companionable as they both dug into their food.

Once they were done and were set to leave. Lilithe took out a tube of lipstick from her purse and coated her faded lips red, once again.

Blaise watched her carefully put it on and commented, "You seem to like the colour red, a lot."

She flashed him a half-smile. "Do I now?"

He pointed to her dark-red purse with gold embroidered roses. And then to her crimson off-shoulder top. "You also thought the redhead woman was beyond beautiful."

Nothing to say to that, she shrugged in admittance.

Blaise pursed in lips, contemplating. "Is that where the moniker Ruby Wraith comes from?"

Lilithe involuntarily stiffens at the mention of it but then tries to play it off. "Well, that and cuz I like it bloody."

The image of her wild curls and bloodied hands flashed past his memory. The pools of scarlet had decorated the room, splashing over pieces of furniture.

His lips unconsciously curled in an unbidden smile. "That you do."

Back then, he was fully preoccupied with the unfolding mystery before him. Thoughts of Lilithe with scared, poison green eyes had filled him. He did not quite have the luxury of musing on what a perfect picture of feral beauty she portrayed; a raw, savage, unrestrained sort of beauty.

Blaise shook himself out of it. Honestly, his thoughts got more and more twisted each day.

"But really." His eyes flew to Lilithe. "Have you ever suspected me of having anything to do with...? Well, before you connected the dots and decided to show up, that is."

Blaise let out a sigh. "Not to that extent. Remember the last time we had dinner at that restaurant?"

Her eyes flashed. "It was that damned TV, wasn't it?"

Blaise blinked, a guilty look on his face. "I am trained to notice these things. You can't blame me, Lily."

"I'm not blaming you," she muttered through her teeth. "I'm blaming my incompetence."

"And from that night, you started ignoring me and I still don't know why," he continued. "Which reminds me, why did you ignore me?"

Lilithe's hand, which was about to put the lipstick back in her purse, stilled. She then let out a chuckle. That came a little too quickly. "I was busy with work." She glanced at him with a smirk. "And I thought I should keep you on your toes."

Blaise docilely nodded as if he bought her excuse but the wheels in his mind kept turning as his sharp eyes continued thoroughly studying her.

Interesting.

Good luck to Blaise on his new mission. He really needs it.

Also these chapters are getting harder and harder to write. I don't know if it's because my writing skills dwindled or because this is new territory for me. I mean, we're over the 'they met for the first time and slowly fell in love!' But now the slow development I have to portray of Lily coming to trust again while also making sure her reactions are realistic and accurate... ugh, the pain.

Anyway, hope you enjoyed this chapter!

Chapter 23

- -

Lily snuck a look at her watch as they finished off their lunch. Her lunch break was over; she needed to head back to her company for a meeting.

As she informed Blaise of that, he calmly guided her to his car, insisting on driving her there.

She quirked an eyebrow at his rare moment of assertiveness - directed at her, that is - but otherwise went along with it. She wasn't losing out on anything. She had ridden a cab here. Waiting for another one would be time-consuming.

He opened the car door, letting her take a seat, before closing it and walking around to the driver's position beside her.

The last time she was in a car with him, she was too preoccupied with... shopping. This time, though, she turned her gaze to him; his side profile.

He was focusing on the road in front. His callous eyes had an edge of concentration. Yet, the expression on his face was relaxed and calm, with a half-smile tugging at his seemingly soft lips.

His hair was messier than it looked on normal days - to be fair, even that was quite messy - like he had been running his hands through it since morning. A stray strand rested on his left eyebrow, just above his eye.

That aforementioned eye glanced at her for a split second before re-focusing on the road ahead. It was so sudden that she didn't have the time to look away and pretend she hadn't been staring at him like all the mysteries of the universe were written all over his face.

Well... she probably wouldn't pay him that much attention if this was the case.

"What's wrong?" His voice came as a murmur.

"Huh?"

"You were staring at me. Do I have something on my face?"

"If I say 'mysteries of the universe', will you believe me?" she asked with good humour.

"I have been pegged as 'mysterious' before so, maybe partially?" His eyes had that amused glint she was used to.

"Oh? By who?"

"Many people," he softly said. "But most meant to be mean-spirited."

"I can't imagine calling someone 'mysterious' maliciously! If I wanted to be cruel, I'd call them... but that's not the point. Mysterious? That's really not..." She trailed off as he let out a deep chuckle.

"Not my vibe?"

"You generally give off an air of... geniality, so to speak. Like you're very friendly and expressive."

"But when they keep spending time with me, Lily, they realize I hide a lot." His eyes flitted to hers again for a moment before focusing back. "Except, that realization always comes a little too late and by that time, I'm already done with them. They outlive their usefulness."

His eyes were clouded with a smidgeon of coldness.

Lily noted it while asking him playfully, "And me? When do you think I'll outlive my usefulness?"

Some of that coldness dissipated. "Let me think... not anytime in the next few decades."

"Decades?" Green eyes, blinking constantly, were staring at him.

The car decelerated, gradually coming to a stop in front of a tall skyscraper. He was silent the entire time, not addressing her bewildered inquiry.

His head turned towards her then. His features arranged in a casual facade. "Why? You don't think we'll be in touch that long?" he raised an elegant brow. "I'm definitely not letting you go."

What...?

Lily blinked at him, trying to process everything that happened in the last couple of seconds. While she took her time, he got out of the car, walked to her side and held open the car door.

She somehow got out without hitting her head on anything. But as she looked at him, dazed, he opened his mouth to ask, "Will you come to my house tonight for dinner."

This was the perfect time to tease him. A distant part of her mind that wasn't malfunctioning thought. She should have peered up at him, slyly, handed him a smirk and asked, "You're missing me already?"

Should have.

Because when she wetted her lips to answer, all that got out was: "We already had lunch together."

... Yeah.

She said something that boring.

His lips twitched. This brat was enjoying this.

However, he languidly tilted his head. "I want to set the table for you. You complained about it last time."

Damnit.

Let a girl have some breathing room, will you?

A light entered his eyes as if he heard her, and decided to disregard her, before he stepped towards her. Closer until they were a few inches apart. "Should I come and get you once you're done?"

The words came in a whisper. And she was having trouble breathing. Like her airways had swelled and narrowed. How come Lily didn't know she was an asthma patient? She needed to check in with a doctor quickly!

She blinked fast and looked away, whipping her hair back behind her shoulders as she discreetly took a huge, calming breath.

"That's alright." Her words came out rushed as she turned away to swiftly walk towards the entrance of her company's building. "I'll be there by myself."

She would bang her head against the wall for this loss of composure later but right now, all she was thinking was how to get away from the vicinity of this man who probably did some dark, ancient witchcraft on her.

As she went into the building through the revolving glass door, she never once looked back.

Lily was greeted by many of the employees as she walked with a purpose towards her office. Or at least, she assumed so based on the usual.

For she didn't currently have the alertness of mind necessary to pinpoint the occurrings of what went on around her. Her mind was in a haze, a cloud of mist and fog, flickering in and out of the reality she needed to be present in at the moment.

The back of her mind registered the dull sound of hurried footsteps following her. There was a muffled voice as well. Someone was talking.

Once she entered her office and sat down on her chair, closing her eyes and steadily exhaling and inhaling led to her finally starting to feel more in balance.

As the fogginess in her mind slowly cleared, the image of her secretary, Cora, appeared in her vision. Cora, who was standing before her, clutching her hands tightly, with a concerned look swimming in her eyes.

"Miss Blackthorne, are you alright? You looked very... out of sorts just now."

Lily glanced at her for a few moments, wondering if she should spill, if only to make sense of every thought swirling in her chaotic mind, before deciding otherwise and asking, "When does the meeting start?"

Knowing she wasn't going to get an answer, Cora bowed her head before replying.

Lily nodded. "Got it, you may leave."

As the door locked behind her leaving secretary, causing a clear silence to streak across the room, Lily slumped down on her chair, boneless. Staring up on the ceiling, Lily could make out the designs etched into it. On first glance it would seem all over the place but the more you stare, the more you see them follow a certain pattern.

Relaxation flowed through her the more sense she made of it. The state of her mind ebbed into the familiar calmness, her delayed thinking process sharpened into its usual quickness until all that remained of the previous catastrophic cacophony was a simple question.

Why?

A simple question indeed but not one with an equally simple answer.

What was it about him?

Why... truly why did she keep on wanting to believe him?

Her eyes fluttered shut as she reached out to pinch the long bridge of her nose, frustration and bewilderment flowing through her veins, spearing a hole through her heart and - a chill travelled up her spine - softening its protective shields.

Chapter 24

If every simple question in the world had an equally simple answer, how great and peaceful would the world be?

Lily's world had been in chaos for the last few hours.

She, who had always been so bold and decisive, never one to hesitate or rethink herself was now rethinking every one of her life choices.

This is it, Selene. She texted. It's over. Let's forget about each other from today. I'm leaving the country.

It took a moment for Selene to reply and Lily pounced on her phone the moment she heard a ping sound.

Bye

... Excuse you?

Not even a 'safe journey'?

She didn't feel like gracing that disgraceful text with a reply so she turned off her phone and shoved it in my purse.

Five seconds later, she grudgingly took out the phone and started texting back: It's just SO embarrassing! I can't ever show my face in public again!!!

In that case, burying yourself might be a better option

Lily let three small dots speak for her this time.

It was a simple advice, Lilithe. You may choose to discard it

YOU'RE NO HELP AT ALL

And down went her phone. Not in the drain, like she thought of doing for a moment, but back into her purse.

Blaise might've looked quite unruffled on the surface but no one was aware of the brewing anxiety that had slowly built up over the past few hours.

He had watched his chef painstakingly prepare a lavish dinner while thinking that food might go to waste. She might not arrive.

He would go and personally pick her up so there'd be no such anxiety but she told him not to. And even if it killed him, he wouldn't do something she didn't want.

He looked at the wall clock. Back to the matter at hand, she might not come.

What if his balancing went slightly off-kilter and she got too scared? He could calculate all he wanted, think of twenty different possibilities of her reactions but he would never be able to predict her thoughts a hundred percent. He might account for ninety-nine percent of it but the one percent that he never could have predicted might occur and take her away from him.

He was already planning all the ways he would coax her to come back to him, wash away her fears when he heard the sound of footsteps making their way towards the dining room.

Standing up from the chair, he turned towards the source of the sounds as his housekeeper led Lilithe to him. As the knots in his heart gradually unlaced, he made a note to give his housekeeper a pay raise.

"You came." The words left his mouth without his permission. His lips pressed together to prevent any other, more compromising or inappropriate, words from escaping. One a day could be considered enough, if he kept throwing Lilithe off balance with too short intervals, the results might be counterproductive.

The raven-haired beauty before him arched an eyebrow, an effortless smile on her red lips. "Who am I to reject free food?"

A hand was placed on her hips as she added, "Didn't you say you were going to set the table for me? Go on, I'm watching."

Her demeanour told him all he wanted to know. His first attempt was a success. The victory brought forth a confident smile on his lips, his mahogany eyes getting shrewder.

As long as the end result came in positive, he was willing to deal with all the uneasiness in the world.

The days from then on went by, more or less, in a smooth manner. His main goal these days had been to take the edge of wariness resting on her shoulders. Every time she arrived at his house, those shoulders seemed a little less burdened. She grew more animated as he let her explore the sprawling mansion as she pleased.

Knowledge was power. And power, for many, meant absolute control. And the woman he thought of day and night was someone who needed control more than anyone else, not just in order to thrive, but also to function like everybody else, free of nightmares and the skeletons in her closet.

The more familiar she was with him and the place he called his home, the more grounded she would feel, the walls she built about her soul, all the more fragile.

The staff in his home grew used to her presence, as such, whenever she arrived, there was little to no fanfare, as if a member of the family had come, instead of a guest.

Therefore, in hindsight, he shouldn't have been so surprised to find her languishing on his chair, concentration on the contents of a file, when he entered his office.

Except that wasn't just any file. That was the file compiled with all the information his illegal background check on her had garnered.

She gave no indication of her noticing his presence by way of her concentration flickering. She continued diligently reading through passages of information about herself.

A silence that was both awkward and ferocious sunk into the room as he leaned against the closed door with his arms crossed, watching her.

"Wow..." She rolled her eyes. Still looking through the contents, looking quite... impressed? "Should I be flattered you went to such lengths to get a detailed idea of me?"

Instead of looking like the picture of guilt, that was to be his initial reaction, he calmly asked, "How did you find it?"

She placed the folder on the smooth, neat desk and glanced at him with a smirk. "You weren't all that inconspicuous with its placement, Blaise. Now, speak: When did you get this done?"

His shoulders relaxed as she didn't seem angry. "Right after we met for the first time."

A chuckle escaped her. "As I guessed, you take no prisoners."

Placing her hands on the desk, she slowly got up from the chair, walking over to the window walls, the sun rays highlighting those black curls, making them seem a mixture of gold and copper.

Peering at her standing under the halo of the soft golden hue, Blaise felt his breath stutter. At that moment, she looked over at him, forest green eyes glinting with something sharp, that seemed to dull as the seconds raced by, until all that was left was a softness that gripped his heart, clenching it painfully, and leaving him utterly breathless in its wake.